Co

Chapter 1 Henry

Chapter 2 Millie

Chapter 3 Katy

Chapter 4 Ra

Chapter 5 Andrew

Chapter 6 The Book

Chapter 7 The boat

Chapter 8. Woods

Chapter 9   Beach

Chapter 10 Library

Chapter 11 Warm

Chapter 12 Home

1

He sat there staring at her waiting for that slight movement.

The sun had been out for a while and that cat had over stayed his welcome.

" Morning handsome I suppose you want me to get up?"

Oh oh she's awake come on get up I have to go outside quick.

Ra rubbed her nose and looked him right in the face. She could see the urgency in his eyes.

" Ok I'm coming."

The covers flew over the bed and her legs curved over the edge.

Henry had gone, pounding down the hallway to the back door.

Ra appeared and went to the kitchen draw for the backdoor key.

Henry couldn't hide his excitement. It may only be the garden but his bladder was screaming to release that pressure and that damn cat was still there.

He shot out the door, RO,RO,RO,RO,RO. The cat looked at this maniac barking at him below. Henry carried on glaring as he weed in his favourite spot.

Ra stood in the window and watched the commotion continue.

" Handbags at dawn I think. Henry you're not going to win."

Henry stood his ground and kept eye contact with this scruffy moggy. It may be some time before this battle was over but he had no other plans for the day so bring it on.

Ra reached out for the kettle and poured the steamy water into her favourite butterfly mug. She grabbed her drink and went outside to the small patio in the garden. It was a warm sunny morning and the garden was full of colour.

A bluetit appeared on the elephant by the roses chittering away looking for some food, bedding who knew.

Ro,ro,ro,ro, Henry shot up the fence teeth gleaming. A clump of fir fell past him. I got him he dropped to the floor turning as he landed to see what else had come down from the fence. Nothing just a piece of fir. Henry looked up at the fence and the scruffy moggy was gone, his eyes lit up with pride. He had won that battle so turned and with his chest puffed out trotted back up the garden.

"Well done you beat him." Ra put her hands out and rubbed the top of Henry's head. He looked up with a big smile.

"I think you deserve a biscuit come on let's see what we have."

Ra headed back in the kitchen followed by a proud black silky Labrador.

An hour had past and Ra was still in her pyjamas. It didn't really matter today she had no plans so could do what she wanted. Well she had no plans for any day. Since her marriage break up she had left her job, moved away from the area in the attempt to make a fresh start around people that didn't know her. Everything had been going well, she had found a lovely little cottage just outside West Brigg. The neighbours an elderly couple were about half a mile down the road and the village was a fifteen minute drive away.

Money was tight but she coped. The main thing is she was safe away from the hideous past life she had endured for 15 years.

"Gosh it's half past twelve and I'm still not dressed. Come on Henry let's get ready and go and explore it's too nice to sulk around here.

She disappeared down the hallway and into the spare room. Henry sat patiently by the door. Finally what seemed to be like hours Ra appeared. She was wearing a grey pair of shorts and a blue t-shirt, in her hand was a grey hoody just in case.

"Now what shall we take to eat, your biscuits and some chews. I'll take some fruit and oh yes let's have them muffins from yesterday."

Henry stood watching as Ra moved around the kitchen collecting items as she went. He couldn't understand what she was doing but he knew when she was done they were going out for a long walk on a beautiful summers afternoon.

His lead jangled as it was taken off the hook.

The front door opened and Henry shot out and ran to the gate. Ra locked the door and checked the latch was locked. She checked it again and again and again.

"I have to do something about this OCD if people could see me they would think I'm mad."

Sure that everything was all locked up off they went heading up the hill towards Kinmel peak.

The sun was at its highest point by the time they reached the top. Ra found a flat spot to sit. Henry flopped down by the side of her panting for cool air. The drinks bottle lid flipped open Ra lent towards Henry and he began to drink. It was so refreshing and cool you could see his breathing slow down and he began to relax.

She wiped the top and began to drink herself. "That feels good. Do you want some biscuits handsome?"

The rucksack unzipped and Henry stood up wagging his tail.

She placed a handful on the fresh grass and his nose dived in to the mix of biscuits.

She looked out over tree tops and watched the magpies and crows go back and forth to their nests. The beech tree seemed to sway to the rhythm of a waltz elegantly from side to side, while the conifer trees were headbanging to their own tune.

"The beauty of this small space seems to get more surprising every time I come here."

Henry jumped and swung round. He stood to attention and glared at the figure in front. It seemed different to what he was used to, he sniffed the air and then grunted.

Ra never flinched she kept looking straight ahead. She didn't want the stranger to see how nervous she was.

"I try to find something different every time I come here. Today I watched the trees dance and it made me feel so humble."

Ra turned to look at who was behind her. What she expected was not what she saw.

In front of her stood a woman. No think special but not ugly.

There was a sense of calmness around them as though they had been in each other's company before.

"You've just recently moved into the village into old ma's cottage?"

Ra was taken back by the comment. Had her husband found out where she had moved to, or even worse her mother in law. No she was being silly it was just local gossip. It was always the same someone new moves into the street and everyone wants to know all their secrets.

"Don't worry it's just local gossip everyone wants to know who you are and where you come from."

"You make it sound like I'm on a game show."

She smiled.

"I'm still trying to get to know people but it will take time."

Henry nudged the ladies hand to let her know he was still there.

"Hello young man well don't you look a handsome chappie." She bent down and run her hand over his head. Henry lifted his head accepting the compliment.

Ra placed the drinks bottle in the side pocket of her rucksack and stood up looking at the view one last time. She knew it wouldn't be the same the next time she came it never was.

"I had better get a move on I haven't done any house work today."

The stranger looked "I'm sorry I didn't mean to disturb you I like to come up here a few times a week it allows me to think in peace."

"Oh no don't be silly it's a good job you did I would have still been here after dusk otherwise."

"If your going back to the village I'll walk with you if that's ok, I haven't had a good conversation today and all that waits for me at home is trudging through assignments."

"You're a teacher then?"

"At the university. I teach Victorian law and principles."

"That sounds intense I don't suppose you have many on that course?"

"I have the largest class on campus and a waiting list.

I am blowing my own trumpet and I like to."

"Very modest and confident I could be like that."

Ra looked at her with a little admiration. She wasn't the kind of person that would stand out from the crowd for her looks but her attitude would allow her to stand at least a foot above everyone else. I wonder what her students thought of her, friend or fo?

"How long have you taught for and have you been anywhere exciting?"

"Oh heavens no I'm not that going to see the world and start a new school in the out skirts of a shanty town in Asia person. I'm happy in the uk. I have been teaching for 25 years but as a professor only 7 years."

The afternoon sun began to hide itself behind the oak trees shedding light on the rose bushes which glowed full of beauty.

"Hello Miss Ventry what a lovely afternoon the memorial garden is screaming full of colour good idea of yours to trim the larches."

" It shows that wonderful view of Bedmans Hill now doesn't it?"

" Until you mentioned that I never really noticed. I suppose I'm just enthralled by the beauty not the view."

"HMNN."

They carried on walking towards the post office at the end of the village.

" This is where I depart. It was a pleasure meeting you."

She turned towards Ra and held out her arms. Ra stood still for a second wondering if this was the right thing to do, they had only just met and this stranger seemed more than comfortable to hug her. Ra leant forward and hugged her. It felt very strange but there was a warmth of serenity there.

" We should meet for coffee are you free Thursday around 11.30 ?"

" I'm always free at the moment. Not thinking of looking for any work at the moment just want to enjoy my freedom."

"Okay Thursday 11.30."

Before Ra could acknowledge she'd turned and gone.

" Well that was an adventure Henry what do think of our new friend?"

Henry looked up tail wagging and eyes gleaming with happiness. Ra slowly walked back up the narrow lane to her home. The sun was still bright and the smell of the foxgloves was relaxing.

Ra began to feel nervous but not sure as to why, nothing was behind her, she wasn't expecting anything to happen.

She shook her head and carried on hoping the feeling would go away.

" Henry why is the gate ajar I'm sure it was locked when we left. It hasn't been that windy."

Henry looked up wagged his tail. As they approached the open gate Henry slowed and begun to huff. He felt there was something wrong and wanted his owner to know. Ra stopped and looked towards the house. Nothing seemed out of place but something didn't feel right.

They both slowly moved towards the front door. Ra removed the keys form her trousers. She began to shake the jangle of the keys suddenly Henry began barking.

A clatter came from inside of the house. Ra dived towards the door and thrust the keys in. The door flung open and Henry dived in searching for the noise.

" Ok ok I'm sorry leave me alone. HELP HELP get this animal of me."

Ra picked up the walking pole she had by the front door and ran towards the kitchen screaming like a banshee. She shot threw the kitchen door and skidded to a halt.

Down on the floor by the sink was a crumpled figure with hands over head mumbling. Henry sat in front and pawed at the figure.

Ra looked down with hands raised ready to leash a sharp blow of pine on whoever it was if they moved. Her heart was pounding and hands shaking but she would not move.

"What do you think gives you the right to enter my home without permission?"

The hands began to move away from the head. Ra clenched the wood ready to swing. A piece of hair dropped down from its clip a pale brow began to emerge raising itself under pressure.

" I'm sorry I just wanted a dry floor to sit on. I haven't broken anything the back door was open, I did call but there was no answer. If you let me have a drink of clean water I will leave you. "

By now a dirt covered face was looking up begging for water. Why water you can get this from anywhere why were they in my house. Ra began to relax her grip but still held the wood above her head.

"Why have you come here surely you can get water from your own home, why break into mine?"

"I have been travelling for over 4 months hiding in the woods or farm buildings as I have travelled. Please don't call the police they will only find out and send me back."

She was shocked who was they, were they running from or being hunted by someone.

"Why are you worried about the police. Is someone after you and why what have you done?"

The figure dropped their head and began to cry.

Ra slowly put down the wood but still in hands reach. She bent down and began to put her hands around their arms.

"Please let me help you up come and take a seat and I'll get you that water."

They slumped into the chair and cried. Henry sat in front of this strange figure trying to understand what he should do.

"Here you go."

A shaky hand reached up and took the slim glass. Ra could see the small green eyes through the matted hair. They seemed dull and tired barely alive.

"What is your name, what are you doing here?"

" I have evaded your home and spoilt your day I'll drink this water and then be on my way."

Ra was shocked by the response she didn't mean to be so heartless just wanted to know who this person was.

"Its ok I'm sorry I didn't mean for you to leave I'm concerned about how you look and what you have said. If your being chased or are in trouble I would like to help if I can."

Henry reached up and placed his paw on their leg. Ra knew she was safe he wouldn't do that if he wasn't sure.

"Your dog is very caring?"

"He tells me when its safe."

"How do you know?"

"I trust him with my life, so should you. You will know if he trusts you."

They raised their head in line with Ra and looked straight at her. She could now see the outline of a thin face with a strong jaw line.

"My name is Katy I lived on the south coast up until 4 months ago. Everything changed and I couldn't cope with it anymore. I left early on a Monday morning and haven't looked back since."

"When was the last time you had a warm drink and proper food? Don't lie or make excuses I can tell from the way you act that you haven't had either for a while. I am happy to help but don't lie to me?"

Ra shot a sharp glare at her warning her to not pull the wool over her eyes.

"Two weeks. I lived of fruit and vegetables for most of the time. The vegetables I have got from farmers fields and fruit of the hedgerows. I don't want to lie to you but I hope you won't ask to many questions as I don't want to tell you to much it may put you off."

"Come on let's get you a hot shower and some clean clothes."

Ra stood up and began to walk to the hallway. She stopped and turned Katy was still sitting at the table drinking her water.

"Come on its getting late you need to get warm."

They made their way to the bathroom. Katy stood in the doorway and stared.

"Are you alright?"

Katy turned to Ra and smiled. Her eyes began to shine with droplets of water. She held out her hand and clasped Ra's left hand.

"Thank you for this after what I have done to you I am blessed."

"Oh don't be silly I'll go and find some clothes for you they may be a little big but they are clean and warm."

Ra turned away and began to close the door. Katy grabbed hold of the door. She shook her head.

The door was left ajar. Katy stood in the bathroom mesmerised by the sun shining into the bathroom. The light bounced of a beautiful glass vase full of sweat smelling yellow roses. She moved forward and sniffed, her heart began to relax and the sweat from her brow slowed down.

She turned on the taps and watched the water cascade into to the tub. It sounded so beautiful. She placed her hand in the water and felt the warmth.

She looked around the room and found a small stool by the window. She began to unbutton her coat it felt so heavy now but she hadn't noticed up until then. Her clothes were folded and place on the stool. She glanced in the mirror the reflection was shocking who was that figure staring back at her. She had not seen her face for days it was not nice.

"Ouch ooh ooh argh. "

She was in. The water surrounded her like a blanket. She began to smile at last she was safe.!

An hour had passed and she was still in the bath. Ra had found a selection of clothes for her try. Some she had never warn. A shopping trip to many she thought.

"Henry do you think she's ok. I can't go in its not right. Tell you what if I give you a treat will you go in and see if she is still alive?"

Henry looked and then huffed. Ra reached for the blue treat tin and took out a tripe stick.

"Now don't eat it yet go into Katy and hand it to her, if she's alive she'll take it out of your mouth and give it back to you. Hopefully she'll get out the bath. I need to see how dirty it is."

Henry took the chew and disappeared down the hallway.

Ra picked up her tea and stood over the kitchen sink the sun had long gone and dusk was taking over. What was she doing a complete stranger had entered her home was now having a bath and wearing her clothes.

Henry appeared in the door dragging his favourite towel.

" Henry your not wet."

He trotted over to Ra and dropped the towel. He sat down and waited.

"Ok if I must."

She grabbed the towel and rapped it him. His head lifted upwards as she rubbed his chest. He groaned and then dropped to the floor and rolled over. Legs in the air Ra carried on rubbing his chest.

Katy finished drying herself of and looked for the largest towel to wrap herself in. She opened the door and headed down the hallway. She peered through the first door the flowers on the window sill filled the room with fragrance. She turned and carried on looking in the rooms to find were clothes would be. The bedroom felt warm and comfy, as with the bathroom the view was jaw dropping. On the bed were clothes laid out neatly. Katy looked and felt she was spoilt for choice. The jeans and grey jumper looked appealing. Her towel dropped to the floor and she picked up the clothes.

"Henry what shall I do for tea, I think we need something like home."

"HUFF HUFF."

He wagged his tail and stood.

"Someone's happy."

Ra looked up and Katy was standing in the doorway. A rush of blood shot to her head. The jeans and jumper looked beautiful why didn't the look like that when she wore them.

"You found something to fit then?"

"Yes thankyou they feel very comfortable. Can I do anything for you?"

"No I'm just thinking of what to do for tea is there anything your not keen on?"

Katy stood for a minute in thought. She'd forgotten what it was like to eat wholesome food so a slice of bread would be wonderful. She looked at Ra and shook her head.

"Ok grab this and go into the garden pick some rosemary and then in this one pick some blackberries and raspberries. Be careful though there is not much room where the bushes are."

Katy took the two containers and disappeared outside.

Ra looked at Henry and flicked her head to oneside.

Henry disappeared out the kitchen door.

It seemed strange to have a someone hunting round her garden. How did she find her it's not as though you can see the house of the road well you can't see it from the fields either. Had she been watching the house or did she just come across it. Why did she run away will someone come looking for her. There were more questions she could ask but they could wait.

"HUFF HUFF" Ra looked up Henry was bouncing round the garden, tail in the air. A twig shot across the soft green lawn and Henry disappeared out of view. Ra smiled she knew Henry could do that all day so Katy would have her hands full.

Katy looked at the herbs in front of her, they all seemed the same. She rubbed the leaves and smelt each one.

"Definitely mint, not sure about that and this one smells likes cats. It's got to be this one it looks pretty."

Katy picked a few sprigs and then went over to the fruit bushes. Henry was rolling on the grass with the twig in his mouth. Ra had peeled some potatoes which were bubbling away on the stove. She opened the fridge and looked inside.

"My god I am spoilt for choice !!!!!not." She pulled out the smoked haddock pieces she had got from village store. It didn't look much but add a few vegetables and it would make a good meal. Katy walked in with two tubs one brimming with fruit the other with sprigs of hopefully rosemary. She held them out in front of her towards Ra.

Ra looked down and smiled. "I take it your not familiar with herbs, that's parsley but not to worry I can use it."

Katy dropped her head she wanted to make a good impression but so far seemed to be doing the opposite.

"Do you like fish I have some smoked haddock. Some boiled potatoes and vegetables and then fruit and fresh cream after we'll have a feast."

Katy smiled and nodded she couldn't remember the last time she he eaten a warm meal. Thinking about it she couldn't remember the last time she felt relaxed. She had broken into to someone's life and evaded their home and she was standing in a kitchen holding fruit and veg in her hands.

The two pots on the cooker started to bubble away Henry sniffed the air he was hoping to get his fair share. Ra looked down at him while she was preparing the haddock.

"Don't worry you won't miss out. Let's get this haddock under grill. Katy can you pass me that spatula of the wall."

Katy looked at the wall at a few utensils hanging on small hooks. She reached out for the green metal spatula and passed it over.

"Is it always this beautiful here?"

"What do you mean by beautiful. I love the smell of fresh air and the garden. I was very lucky the garden was already like this when I moved in. It was one of the reasons why I brought it."

"What was the other reason?"

"Privacy the house is very secluded and can't been seen from the road or the fields. I am surprised that you found the house."

Katy looked she didn't understand what Ra was trying to say. Did she think that she had been spying on her. Well the answer to that was no she didn't know how she found her way here she just kept on walking and then the house appeared. It was like a fairy tale when she saw it.

She turned and looked at Ra. "I am truly sorry for what I have done. I only wanted to feel warm and dry for a while. It's been so long since I felt relaxed."

"I have to say I was ready and prepared to have a go at whoever was in here. You don't expect to get home after a lovely relaxing day to find someone sitting on your kitchen floor."

Ra began to snigger at the sight of what she saw and Henry pawing at her head. She reached over to the pan of potatoes on the cooker and pronged one of the potatoes.

"Ok food is ready can you get some plates out of the cupboard in the corner and then get Henry's bowl from the side as well. Katy collected the plates and the bowl and placed them on the table.

Henry sniffed the air and licked his lips. They all sat at the table and tucked in.

Katy slowed as she ate. The food was wonderful but eating it quickly would show how hungry she really was. She wanted to enjoy and remember the taste of her first hearty meal in months.

"I have to say this is wonderful. I know I haven't eaten like this for a long time, thankyou."

Tears began to run down her face. Ra looked and then looked away. What should she do nobody had ever cried while eating her food. It must have something to do with why she ran away, but she couldn't ask Katy had already made it clear that this was something she didn't want to talk about.

"Ok are you ready for fruit pie and cream?"

The pie was still nice and warm as it was sliced. Within 10 minutes the plates were clean. Henry sat waiting for his cream. Ra poured a little into her dish and placed it on the floor. Henry slurped away until the bowl was clean.

"You must let me wash and dry the crocks up I insist."

Ra looked and smiled she hated cleaning up after cooking so that was a nice surprise.

"You do that then and I'll make some tea.

Silence fell as both got on with what they were doing.

Katy seemed to take time washing up. Ra couldn't decide whether it was nerves or the enjoyment of soaking her hands in warm water.

The kettle began to whistle Ra reached for the tea towel and turned off the gas. The water hissed as it fell into the pot.

The clean crocks glistened on the side. The different colours bounced off the walls like a rainbow.

Ra picked up the tray and headed towards the sitting room.

Katy looked up she was still drying her hands. She dropped the towel on the side and quickly rushed towards the door.

Even though she was indoors she still felt nervous could there be someone lurking in the bushes watching her waiting for her to be alone. She shivered and shook her head.

"Would you like sugar and milk in your tea?"

She looked puzzled why did she not answer her. She just stood there looking at the fire place.

Ra poured herself a cup of tea and then sat down. Katy still stood staring.

"What's the matter you haven't moved for the last 5 minutes. I dusted this morning before I went out so it can't be that untidy."

Katy seemed to come round from her trance and back to the present. She came and sat in the chair opposite Ra.

"Help yourself to tea and biscuits its easier that way. I can always put more water in the pot."

Katy picked up the pot and it nearly slipped forward. She quickly placed it back on the table and re arranged her grip and tried again.

A few minutes had gone by and nobody spoke. Henry lay by the fire in front of them both. He looked up and then huffed.

Why was it so quiet she didn't have visitors so having someone there should me the air full of voice.

"Why did you move down here?"

How do I answer that. Do I tell her the truth or not. How do I know she hasn't come to spy on me. I don't know who she is or where she has really come from or what has happened to her. It could all be a pack of lies.

"Let's just say my life and circumstances changed . I needed somewhere new to start again. I noticed this house for sale in one of the country magazines so put in an offer."

"Didn't you come and take a look at it before you brought it?"

"No. I liked the floors came and spoke to a few of the village folk to ask about the house. What they told me about it sounded wonderful so I put in an offer and it was snapped up. Couldn't believe it really because I offered below the original asking price. Must have wanted a quick sale."

Katy looked at her.

"Was it all you thought it would be when you got here "

"I was pleasantly surprised. I had to do a little decorating but the building is very stable. It was an elderly couple who lived here. I was told their names were Ada and Frank.

Frank died of a heart attack about 8 years ago and Ada passed away last year. I was told the village council tried to find out if they had any family still alive."

"Did they?"

"They mentioned something about a possible granddaughter but they weren't sure. Sad really they say their only daughter was involved in a boating accident when she was 7 months pregnant."

"What happened to her was she on her own.?"

"Don't really know, nobody said. I presume she died."

Katy dropped her head. Such a sad end to the story.

The light was fading in the sitting room Ra stood and walked over to the standard lamp by the side of the fire.

Katy blinked as the light shone she had not been used to it.

The room looked cosy. She could imagine how comfortable it would feel with the fire roaring away in the winter.

"I don't know what's on the tv I only really watch the news or gardening. Don't like the soaps much makes you feel depressed all they while.

"I never watched much telly at home I was always outside. Could never see the point of staying in when you could enjoy the beauty of what each day holds ahead."

"Very philosophical for someone so young!"

Ra smiled as she spoke. The children she knew were always on their mobile phones or play stations.

"Well let's have a look at the news see what's going on.

Ra reached for the remote on the side table and pressed the green button. The screen flickered while it was warming up and then the picture appeared. She flicked through the channels until the news appeared. The news reader was a middle aged man with a blue stripped suit and green tie. They both sat quiet for a moment listening to what atrocities were happening in the world.

The Russians were bragging about their armies, americans accusing the rest of the world of hating them and the Asian countries struggling to survive due to floods, earthquakes and famine. There were numerous adds for donations for different causes. Ra tutted.

"We have some breaking news coming to us from the Cornish coast." Their heads shot up.

"We are getting reports of a boating accident near the town of Pencracken. The report states that a small sail boat has washed up with no persons aboard. At the moment there have been no reports of anyone missing. The police are trying to find out who is the owner of boat. We will bring you more on this story when we have an update.

"I hope whoever was on there are safe somewhere. Surely there is a name on the boat all boats have a name."

Katy sat still not looking away from her cup. Ra could see the coy look on her face. Was she anything to do with the boat. Did she know who the boat belonged to.

"You come from Cornwall is that anywhere near where you lived?"

"Oh no we were further round the coast. I don't think I have ever been to that village I have heard of it though. Do you mind if we have more tea?"

Ra shook her head picked the tea pot up and disappeared into the kitchen.

The kettle wasn't warm enough so she relit the gas and placed the kettle back on the stove. She emptied the used teabags into the compost bin and placed 3 fresh ones in the pot. She stood looking out of the window but it was too dark to see anything. She could still hear the robins chattering away.

Henry came into the kitchen and went straight to the back door. Ra walked to the door and pulled it open. He disappeared outside tail in the air.

She returned to the stove and lifted the kettle.

"I think it's going to be a chilly night tonight. If you want any extra covers for the bed just let me know."

She placed the tray on the table and began to pour tea into Katy's cup.

"There you go nice and hot."

She looked up and the slim figure in front of her was curled up on the chair. Was she a sleep or………..no of course she wasn't she was definitely a sleep. She sat back down picked up her tea and sipped in silence. Henry came in wagging his tail.

"Another half an hour and I think we'll turn in what do say?"

"Would you mind if I go now I can't keep my eyes open?"

Ra turned how long had she been awake for. Had she been watching her while she was drinking her tea.

"No carry on. If you need anymore blankets there in the cupboard on the right just before your bedroom."

Katy got up rubbed the top of Henry's head and disappeared.

Silence filled the room. Doubt began to rise would she be safe, would she still be here in the morning, would everything still be there.

" Come on lets go."

Henry jumped up and disappeared into kitchen. Ra placed the tray on the side. Henry went to his toy box and picked out his hedgehog. The nose was gone and the prickles were minimal but he loved it. Ra walked towards the spare room and stopped. She couldn't hear anything. She was tempted to open the door and check she was ok but thought better of it.

She disappeared into the bathroom and turned on the tap. 5 minutes later she was undressed and getting in to bed.

Henry went to his bed and circled until he was comfortable.

The house went silent.

Would she still be here when she woke up tomorrow, would she take anything while she was a sleep? Who was she really why did she turn up at her house. Why was she thinking like this?

"Stop thinking like that you've been watching to many American detective programs. Henry looked up and then dropped his head.

Every noise that she was used to seemed to sound louder than normal. How can having someone else in the house make her feel so nervous. She seemed very genuine or was this a ploy.

Ra sighed and then turned over and faced the window. She could hear the bushes rustling from the wind and she could see the light reflecting on the lantern outside the front door.

But it was still quiet.

2

Henry woke up and grumbled. He looked towards the door waiting to see if it was going to open. Ra was still asleep he had to be sharp and ready for whatever came through the door. The door handle pushed down and began to move towards him. He stood up and growled come on bring it on his head dropped and he crouched.

Frozen to the spot his eyes were glued to the door.

A hand stretched around the door and a head began to appear. Katy looked over at Ra still asleep and then glanced at Henry. She waved at him and then began to close the door.

Henry ran towards the door and put his head in the small gap that was getting smaller. Katy turned round she couldn't shut the door to see his head looking up at her.

"Henry I am sorry I didn't know you were there. Do you want some water? Come on let's get breakfast started."

They both disappeared into the kitchen.

The sun was just rising and the birds were jumping around the garden looking for seeds. A squirrel was rummaging through the leaves that had been raked up.

Henry stood by the back door wagging his tail.

"Hang on a minute let me open the door for you."

Katy walked towards the door grabbed the handle and turned it. Nothing happened. She looked down at his handsome face.

"It's locked where is the key ? Do you know ?"

Henry turned and headed towards the corner dresser at the back of the kitchen and nudged the handle.

Katy opened the draw and there they were. A set of four keys with a daffodil keyring. She walked towards the door and tried two keys before she found the one that fitted.

She pulled the door ajar and Henry shot outside barking at anything that moved. Where was it where had the cat from the other day had it come back for more or decided to keep a safe distance.

Katy looked shocked and began to panic. Ra wasn't awake yet and she didn't want her to be disturbed.

"Henry sshh please be quiet she is not awake yet."

Henry took no notice and carried on marshalling the garden borders waiting for something to appear. There was something there he knew it he could sense it. Come on show yourself be brave.

"Don't worry he does that every morning. The squirrels come from down the forest when the berries are ripe. I think he seems to think he will catch one."

Katy jumped and looked behind her. Ra was standing there in her peach and grey pyjamas. Strangely she looked very attractive. Her mousy blonde hair hanged loosely to one side And her green eyes shone against the sun that began to appear through the window.

"Would you like tea or coffee?"

Ra smiled at the person standing in front of her. She could see that Katy wanted to do whatever she could to repay the kindness that she had been shown but she was set in her ways and wanted it to stay that way.

"Why don't you go and calm Henry down, he is just looking for something to justify why he's running around like a mad man and I'll sort out breakfast."

Katy looked at Ra with shock. What had she done, was Ra going to tell her to get her belongings and leave.

"I'm just set in my ways, I like to start my day in a certain way. You haven't done anything wrong don't panic.

Katy gave out a sigh of relief and then disappeared out into the garden. Henry looked over from the hedgerow wagging his tail. He looked at the privet then at Katy telling her there was something there and she needed to come and see.

"What's the matter Henry what's there. Henry began to stamp his paws and looked at the privet. Katy put her hand on Henry's back and looked through the gap. She began to smile and the stroked Henry.

"Who's a good bye what have you found? Shall we go and find a box to put him in?"

Henry wagged his tail and looked at Katy. Where is she going you can't just walk away and leave me with this animal what do I do if it moves how do I stop it. Henry looked shocked as Katy began to walk away.

Katy walked towards the kitchen and it hit her. Bacon, sausage, eggs coffee, toast. It was wonderful the smile could not have been wider as she walked into the kitchen.

"I take it your hungry then. What is Henry getting excited about, its not the cat is it I thought it would have learnt its lesson after last time."

"Oh no he's found a baby hedgehog. Would you happen to have a box of some kind that I can put it in?"

Ra stood silent for a moment. Where or did she have any boxes available. Oh yes she had the boxes from the fruit delivery from the other week.

" If you go towards the log store behind it you will find a metal container. Look inside and there should be some card board boxes."

" Ok thank you."

Katy disappeared back into the garden and headed towards the log store. Henry was still glued to the spot. This object was not going to get away.

She looked behind the log store and found an old rusty bin. She lifted the lid and found inside some different sized boxes.

Henry still looked at the object which hadn't moved.

"Ok Henry lets get this little fellow to safety. We don't want you get hurt by his spikes."

Henry grunted as he moved away. Katy placed the box on the floor and with a twig she had picked up from by the log store she began to roll the hedgehog towards the box.

They both made their way back to the house, Henry trotting of in front with his tail in the air.

"Have you got him?"

"Yes I was going to check him over if that's ok. He doesn't seem very old I don't know if he has been left or abandoned by his mother. Is there somewhere or can go to take him out of the box?"

"There's a small laundry room at the back of the kitchen you check him out in there. If you look in the cupboard on the left as you go in you'll find some old rags throw it away when you have used it."

Katy smiled and disappeared into the next room. The hedgehog seemed peacefully asleep it was a shame to wake him but she needed to know if he was ok.

The rag she found was quite thick so she wouldn't need to put on gloves. She placed the small creature on the top and began to carefully examine the small creature. Slowly he seemed to wake and his small paws began to stretch showing soft pink pads. Katy smiled this little fellow was fine now she had to find some food.

She came back into the kitchen with the box and headed towards the door.

"Where are you taking him?"

"Back to where I found him I can keep him safe outside in the box. I just need to find him some food there should be plenty of worms and snails about. I think he is old enough to eat that kind of food if not I can mash up some scrambled egg or some fruit."

Katy disappeared outside followed by Henry. Ra looked out of the window and watched as they both went behind the hedge. She walked over to the side table and picked two plates up. She began loading the plates with bacon, sausage and scrambled eggs. The kettle had boiled and she poured the water in.

"Is he safe now?"

"We will have to see I have left him with a snail in the box so I will check on him later."

"Come on take a seat and have some breakfast."

The kitchen went quiet as the ate breakfast.

Ra looked out the window it was going to be another lovely day so let's see what excitement today will bring. Oh no it's Thursday she had arranged to meet Miss Ventry for coffee in the village. What was she to do. She couldn't not turn up that would look very ignorant, but what about her un announced visitor she couldn't leave her on her own in the house she doesn't know much about her or what she would do.

What a dilemma. She carried on eating breakfast but seemed to have began to eat a little quicker.

"Are you hungry or do you have to be somewhere?"

"What?"

Ra turned and looked at Katy she had a worried look on her face.

"Sorry I have just remembered that I promised to meet one of the villagers I had met on Tuesday for coffee today."

"Go I won't get in your way. If you want me to go I will I can carry on and find the next village to get some food or shelter. I have done it for the last few months so it won't be a problem. After the way I gained entry to your property I can't expect you to let me stay. "

Ra sat sipping her tea. Should she let her stay or kick her out to go and fend for herself somewhere else. She couldn't it was not in her nature.

"I tell you what you can stay I won't say anymore as I don't want to insult you."

Katy looked straight into her eyes. The warmth of her smile made her feel she was at home. There was no way she could ever do any wrong to her. She jumped out her chair and wrapped her arms around Ra and hugged her.

"Thankyou so much I promise you will never regret this you will have to do nothing. When you get back everything will be done."

They both put the breakfast plates by the side of the sink.

Ra headed for the bedroom to get changed and Katy began to wash up the crocks. Henry sat by his bowl waiting for the bacon rind that had been left on the plates. Katy looked down at him and smiled. She had never felt so happy to be able to wash up in a kitchen again.

Ra appeared back in the kitchen. She had changed into her peach t-shirt and pale blue shorts.

"Very nice perfect for this summers day. Is it ok if I give Henry the bacon rind?"

Henry sat patiently dribble running from the left side of his mouth. Ra looked down and smiled it wouldn't be nice to refuse him a little treat so she nodded her head. The bacon was gone within seconds Henry looked to floor just in case he dropped any but no the floor was clean.

Ra looked the clock she should get going it would take her about 20 minutes to walk to the village and she wanted to get there a little early. Nerves began to tingle was she doing the right thing leaving a stranger alone in her house. It was to late now she had said she could stay.

"Ok I had better get going are you sure you'll be ok?"

"I promise I won't do anything I have Henry to keep me an eye on me. Now go have a good time it will do you good to let the villagers see who the new person is stop all the gossip don't you think?"

She was right at the villagers would be able to put a face to the name. She walked towards the door and turned to see Henry sitting by the kitchen why was she not holding his lead was she leaving him will he never see her again he was worried. Ra turned and bent down Henry ran towards her. She fussed him and smiled.

"I won't be long I'm just going to see a friend Katy will be with you don't worry."

Henry looked up he wasn't happy she could tell but he knew she would be back. She rubbed to top of his head and the turned and went out of the door.

Henry sat there she was gone.

"Henry come on lets go and check to see if the hedgehog see if he is still there."

He didn't move. Katy walked up to Henry and put her hand on his head.

"She is coming back I promise you. Come on let's go outside."

Henry looked up at the face it wasn't his mom he didn't want to go he wanted to wait she said she wouldn't be long.

Katy turned and walked away leaving him on his own. Now what should he do sit there and be stubborn or follow her and see what she was going to do.

Come on let's go he stood up and trotted off to the kitchen, she wasn't there. He disappeared out into the garden the sun was shining over the shed and he could smell the fresh pine trees. A noise came from behind the shed and Henry disappeared.

"Hello I wondered how long it would take for you to come and find me. Look the hedgehog has gone so I hope he is ok.

Now what can do let's have a look does the garden need a tidy up."

She could see nothing out of place but this was what she was expecting. She headed back to the house, she may as well have look to see if anything needs doing there but she wasn't holding out any hope.

She walked around the house and found nothing. Everything was in its place and she could see no dust anywhere. How long does she spend on cleaning it must take up most of her day, no wonder she doesn't go out. Katy smiled and went back into the kitchen. Henry was sitting outside watching the birds flit from one rose tree to the next.

"Henry what shall we do, do you want to go for walk."

His ears pricked up, what had she said. Did she really say walk? Before Katy could move Henry ran in the kitchen and stood by the wash room door.

A few minutes later Katy had checked all the doors were locked and of down the drive they went.

"Ok Henry which way do we go. Come on let's go to the village we might see your mom. I don't think I've been to this village."

There was a slight breeze as they walked passed the meadows. The beautiful smell of the rapeseed plants came across there path, they both sniffed the air.

Ra entered the village and immediately felt a hundred eyes stare at her. She was the new villager that everyone wanted to see. Some of the villagers smiled at her a she went by and then huddled in groups and began gossiping. She didn't look back, she didn't people to see if she was concerned about being talked about. She came to the café door and looked in to see if she could see her guest.

"I couldn't have timed that any better come on let's go in before we have a crowd standing outside."

Ra turned around and there she was. She looked over her shoulder and could see the few people standing over the road watching as they went in.

"Hello Millie usual table. Who's this we have here?"

"Hi my names Ra I have just moved into the cottage at the top of the lane."

Ra put out her hand and clasped the hand in front of her.

Millie looked at little surprised at the confidence Ra had showed. They went and sat at a small round table towards the corner of the café by the window.

"Ok what would you like or shall I leave to browse the menu."

"Yes please can I get my tea and what would you like to drink Ra?"

"I'll have an earl grey please."

The waitress disappeared and Ra began to study the menu.

Smoked salmon bagel with summer salad and crusty bread,

Avocado salad with walnuts, roast beef on rye and pumpkin seed bread. This didn't seem like a usual café menu.

"I think I will have the roast beef today the bread is to die for what takes your fancy Ra my treat."

"Oh that's very kind of you. I think I'll go for the smoked salmon please."

Millie put up her arm and the waitress came over pen and pad ready. She ordered the food and place the menus back into the wooden carved holder.

"Do you think I'm what they expected?"

Millie looked out the window just as two middle aged women walked passed.

"I wouldn't worry it won't last something will happen to take their minds of you. Anyway what have you been doing since we last met, had any visitors?"

Ra sent a sharp glance towards Millie how did she know about Katy nobody came past the house. God people were nosy round here she would have to be careful.

The waitress brought the tea and placed it on the table.

Ra picked up the cups and saucers and placed them on the table. There was only one teapot and she had ordered earl grey.

"Did you have earl grey aswell?"

"Yes that's my usual. You can play mother I only take a little milk and no sugar please."

Ra carried on and poured away. The steam rose from the cups and the sent was sharp and crisp.

They both seem to stir at the same time. Ra smiled to herself she hoped Millie wasn't looking.

"Here we go ladies hope you enjoy.

The food looked desirable and plentiful.

"I don't know where to start it looks beautiful."

The table went quiet as they consumed their meals.

The village outside seemed to be getting busier. Ra looked at the visitors stood admiring the flowers and displays outside the shops. They did look beautiful she had to admit.

Oh that woman looked like Kate. What was she doing in the village there was nothing wrong was there, had she burnt the house down, was Henry ok or was she being silly.

Should she go out to her. No she couldn't just get up and leave it would be ignorant.

"Are you ok you seem a little agitated. "

She looked over at her but said nothing. Henry had gone out of site. Her rate began to slow.

"I'm fine I thought I spotted someone I knew but they have gone. I have to say that food was amazing would you like some more tea?"

MMilie nodded but never spoke.

Why had she come into the village was there something wrong, was she looking for her or was she just getting fresh air.

The sun was high in the sky as they left the café the smell of the honeysuckle and phlox filled the village. There were still a few visitors walking along the footpaths looking in the shop windows admiring the displays.

Ra smiled she was now part of this village maybe she should look for something to do see what groups are available. It was about time she stopped hiding and meet people.

"I have to say the warmth of the sun on my face makes me feel so lucky to live here."

Millie turned and looked at Ra. A bit of a strange comment but she could understand what she meant that is exactly how she felt when she moved to the village 18 years ago.

"Well thankyou for joining me today I know we haven't spoke much but a few hours away from those papers makes me feel human."

"I suppose it takes a long time to mark them?"

"Marking is fine its all the typing I have to do my fingers aren't that good these I have the onset of arthritis so I can only do so many at a time. The students are beginning to get a little fed up with the time they to wait."

"I can help if you want it's not as though I am in undated with work and getting me out the house will."

Millie looked in front but never said a word. Had she said something wrong. Was Millie that independent that it was against her principles to accept help from anyone let alone the newbie in the village.

"Actually I have to say that sounds a jolly good idea when can you start?"

"I need to sort something out with Henry but that will only take a few days."

"Bring him with you I have plenty of room and I'm sure I can find him something to play with. How about coming over to mine on Thursday not to start but just to get to know what you are letting yourself in for?"

Ra looked. "Ok that sound fine what's your address?"

"Wonderful I live at The Furrs it's the house at the end of the village entrance. Just as you come into the village you will see a road on your right, follow it to the end and you'll see the house in front of you. "

"Ok what time about 10.30 am would that be ok?"

"That sounds fine gives me chance to tidy up a little I'm not the tidiest person."

"Don't worry about that I'm not a prude."

Ra looked over and spotted a smirk. They said their goodbyes and went off to their homes.

It had been a good day so far today the food was lovely it was nothing like she had expected from a café.

"Well I say my goodbyes and see you tomorrow."

Ra smiled and nodded.

They both went their separate ways. The sun was beginning to lower behind to trees but it was still warm.

Ra admired the freshly cut fields and the clean smell. It was days like this she knew she had made the right choice to leave she turned up the small drive towards the cottage the smell of the rosemary and catmint was strong.

" Ruff ruff."

Ra looked up pounding down the path came Henry his eyes wide and mouth open, he barged the gate open causing it to bang against the stone wall. She bent down and out stretched her arms. It had been a long time since he had greeted her like this. He jumped at her sending her backwards, his tail wagging and tongue washing every part of her hands.

"Ok ok I'm happy to see you too now come on let me get up of this dirty floor when Henry moved back still excited but allowed Ra to get up. They both headed towards the cottage.

At the door stood Katy smiling.

"I had to let him out otherwise head scrapped a hole through the door. He so loves you I have never seen a dog so happy to see someone come home.

"I have put the kettle on would you like a cup of tea?"

"That sounds lovely but I think I need to get changed first, I am a little messy don't you think?"

Ra turned around to see the big dirty patch and the back of her shirt. Katy laughed as they both headed through the door. Henry had disappeared into the kitchen to his bowl.

Ra carried on into the bathroom as Katy followed Henry into the kitchen.

"That was quick I haven't poured the tea yet."

Ra walked over to the table and sat down. Katy brought over the tray and placed it down.

"Why did you come into the village today?"

Katy stopped pouring and looked up at her. She felt as though she had been caught taking the apple from the tree. She began to pour the tea.

"I didn't want to stay in the cottage on my own. It was a lovely day so I thought I would have a look. It has been such a long time since I mingled with people I wanted to know how it felt. I have to say the village is beautiful isn't it so full of flowers. I was surprised to see so many visitors I didn't know it was such a popular village."

"Visitors stop here before they carry on to Scotland. This is the time of year all the shop keepers make their money. We do still have visitors through the year but not as many."

"Do you have a job?"

"I didn't until today. The lady I had lunch with has asked me to help her. She is a professor at the University."

"I didn't know there was a university near here?"

"I'm not sure which university she teaches at I didn't ask. I'll find out tomorrow. She wants me to type up the reports as she has arthritis in her hands. She said the students get a little impatient when having to wait for their notes."

Suddenly Ra began to think about tomorrow. It wasn't the fact that she was going to start a new job it was Henry, her home and Katy. What was she to do. Katy hadn't said how long she intended to stay for if she would allow her to. Henry hadn't been alone since she had moved would she be able to take him with her. Could she trust to leave a stranger in her home un supervised for such a long time. She looked at Katy who was pouring the tea. She seemed happy. How long had she been travelling, was someone looking for her she did say that she had run away. What would happen if someone did find her and force to go home, what if they trashed her cottage or hurt Henry.

Why was she thinking like this she should be happy with how today went. Not only had she made a friend she had got herself a job a chance to earn a little money to keep her going.

"Katy I do have a concern about me taking this job."

Katy looked up unsure of what to expect. She looked nervous it was to late to back out now Ra had to say what she thought.

"You must understand that Henry and my home are very important to me. Even though you have caused me no concern since you have been here I don't know that much about you and also what your intentions are?"

The kitchen went quiet Ra looked at her cup and sipped her tea. Katy sat and looked at Ra it was very uncomfortable but she had the right to know why she had run away from home and why she had come to her house in specific.

"I am very grateful for you allowing me to stay at your home and it is true I do owe you a full explanation."

Katy took a sip of her tea and then a deep breath.

Ra began to feel very nervous and her body began to tingle.

Would she be able to cope with what she was about to hear or was it a mistake that she had said anything at all.

"It is true that I ran away from home. I lived in Turbridge for 23 years and for most of it I was happy. But just over a year ago a family moved into the village. They were a middle aged couple with 2 teenage children boy and a girl. They seemed very nice and polite at first. The father was tall and chunky with dark short hair and the wife was short a little chubby with medium length brown hair. The children were slim and boring looking really."

"Did they work or were they retiring down there?"

"As far as I was told they had their own business but I don't know what they did. I began to notice that something wasn't right about 4 months after they had arrived. There were some people turning up in the village and they didn't fit in. They would not speak to anyone and they were very ignorant when they came into the shops. It was as though we had stop what we were doing and concentrate on them and only them. A few times I asked who they were and was told not to get involved. Well that made me even more inquisitive so I did the exact opposite. One afternoon I followed one and they went to the new family home. I couldn't see much but what I did wasn't right."

Ra leaned on the table and hugged her cup. This was intriguing she had to know more. Katy sipped her tea and looked at Ra. She could see the interest in her eyes should she tell her everything even though it may change how she will feel about her. She had to tell her after the kindness she had shown.

"There seemed to be a lot of people at the home. The funny thing was none of them had been seen coming through the village to get to the house. You see there is only one way in and one way out. But then I thought the house was only a few minutes walk from the beach but people would notice if boats came in and out. I did mention it to my father but he didn't seem interested."

"Have you actually spoken to any of them?"

"I have tried but they just look at you and walk past. The last time I spotted any of them in the village was a week before I left. It was the son he seemed to be away with the fairies.

He was muttering to himself and shaking his head. He nearly bumped into Marven by the post office."

"Did you speak to your dad about leaving or did you just go?"

"I did tell him I was thinking of moving away from the village to try and better myself. There was no work for me well not what I wanted to do anyway. Standing in the post office for 8 hours a day didn't appeal to me."

"What is it your looking to do?"

"Actually now I think about it when I did speak to him he just smiled and said I would never leave because I was too weak."

Ra looked ahead at the figure in front of her. Should she ask her if she feels upset or just sit and listen. One thing she should do is call Henry in and close the door it was dark and the temperature was dropping.

She walked to the door and looked outside. Henry was sitting by the bush where they had found the hedgehog.

Henry come on lad time to put the world to bed."

Henry turned and trotted back to the kitchen. She patted his head as he came in. He looked up with a smile and then went to Katy for the same.

"I'm having a coffee would you like one?"

Ra turned to see her leaning on the table head in hands.

"Katy would you like a coffee?"

Katy looked up and smiled. Ra took this as a yes and lifted two cups of the shelf.

"Come now don't worry about something that has already happened its gone."

Ra placed two steaming cups of coffee followed by the milk and sugar. The aroma was warming. Katy reached for the cup and took a sip her lips curled and nose puckered. Ra smiled and watched as Katy reached for the milk and then slipped a spoon of sugar in. She tried it again and gave a sigh. That was better.

"Do you want to join me in the sitting room I like to watch the secret garden."

Ra stood up and headed for the sitting room. She didn't look back to see if Katy was following. It might be best to leave her with her thoughts for a while.

"I wonder if I could get some of that round here."

"What's that something for the garden I wouldn't have thought you have the room anyway it's beautiful as it is."

"Oh it's to go out the front. I'm looking for a small tree or bush that flowers and smells amazing. I want visitors to get an idea of what they will see in the garden."

"Ooh what were you thinking off?"

"Well on the secret garden just they have just showed Pineapple Broom and Viburnum. I might have to go into the city though I don't think the local shops or even Johnsons garden centre will have them. I'll call Johnsons tomorrow just to check. Are you ok?"

"Yes, since I left I never actually thought about what my dad had said and how he said it. He made me think that he wasn't really bothered whether I or stayed or went. It makes you feel a little unwanted opens up a whole you never thought was there."

Ra just sat drinking her know cold coffee, she didn't know what to say how could she.

"I tell you what how about we get showered and changed and we'll walk into the village and have a drink at the Bumble. What do you say?"

Henry's ears pricked up was he going to go out again today.

Ra bent down to him and rubbed his head. He was going she only did that when she was going to get ready and they were going walking.

They both disappeared into their individual rooms.

Henry sat in the hallway waiting to see which door opened first. He sat there and sat there and sat there then he lay down. Waiting seemed hard work and very boring if they don't hurry up this pooch will be asleep.

Ra and Katy both stood in front of their mirrors deciding what they were wearing was good enough. It was though they were dressing for a local ball not a drink in the village pub.

Ra shrugged her shoulders and opened the door. She walked into the hallway and there he was snoring away. Katy followed a few seconds behind. She stood by Ra and looked down the hallway. He looked so cute sleeping by the kitchen door. Should they leave him there and go out on their own no it wouldn't be fair he was part of the family, he welcomed her into the family the same as Ra did.

"Henry come on let's get your lead were going for a walk."

The blob of fur shot up in the air and took on all different shapes before it looked like a living object.

Will you get his lead and check the back door is locked I will check the windows in the bedrooms."

Katy look at Ra puzzled, why would she have too check the windows none of them had been opened all day. Ra disappeared into her bedroom.

By the time Katy had got Henry on his lead and checked the back door was closed Ra was waiting at the front door.

3

The sun had gone in but it still felt warm. Henry trotted on in front smelling every bush and wetting every tree.

Ra and Katy chatted about anything and everything. It would have felt a very long walk if they had not spoken.

They approached the start of the village high street and could hear loud conversation and laughing. This was unusual as the shops and cafes were closed and the coaches full of tourists would have left.

"Henry come on let's put your lead on now."

He stopped and sniffed the air. Something smelt exciting ahead, he wanted to investigate but knew he would have to behave.

Ra clipped his lead to his collar and then carried on towards the pub.

As they got closer the noise seemed to be coming from the pub. Was there a special event if so she hadn't seen any adverts for it.

"Hi didn't expect to see you down here have you come to celebrate the Wilmlows first born? "

Ra turned and behind her stood Millie. She looked startled more than surprised. Millie didn't seem to be the kind of person to attend this kind of get together.

Katy stood looking between them both listening to quick conversation between them. Who was this woman? Is this the lady Ra had been talking about. She was nothing like what Ra had described, she was expecting a tall extravagant lady, but instead there was a medium build average height lady who seemed to have a strong presence about her.

Millie finally looked towards her and smiled as she leaned forward to fuss Henry. The air fell silent for a few seconds.

Henry nudged Millie's hand for another head rub he felt he deserved. Milly rubbed his head and smiled. Henry was happy and carried on walking along side Ra.

They arrived at the pub entrance and could see it was a little full.

"Why don't you take Henry into the beer garden and I will get the drinks?"

Katy pointed towards the bar and followed Millie.

Ra nodded and disappeared. Millie and Katy headed for the door. The pub was full but they managed to find their way to the bar quiet easily.

"What would you like Millie?"

"Hello Tom can I get a pint of lager shandy, large glass of red wine and my usual please?"

Tom nodded and grabbed the glasses. Two minutes later three glasses sat on the bar. Millie paid and received her change.

They both headed outside to the beer garden. Even though it was busy Ra seemed to have found a table.

"How did you manage to get a seat I would have thought you had no chance with the amount of people who are here?"

"Just luck I suppose."

They all sat down and took a sip of their drinks.

Nobody spoke it didn't seem right. The atmosphere was full of happiness, laughter and love.

Two men were standing by the gate looking at a photo, a young woman was playing with a child's hair trying to make it look smart.

The village hadn't seen this much jollity in a long time.

"Are you ok you seem a little edgy?"

Katy turned and looked at Millie. She seemed to looking at her. But why had she done something.

"I'm fine just making sure nobody treads on Henry he has a habit of lying in the most awkward places."

A few more people came through the rear gate and headed straight back into the pub.

Ra looked as a couple sniggered and hid their heads in their hands.

"Are you still ok for tomorrow?"

Ra looked blank for a moment. What was she doing tomorrow, what day was it tomorrow?

The she clicked. "Oh yes absolutely I will bring Henry as well if that is still ok?"

Katy looked but said nothing.

Millie finished her drink and licked her lips. She looked up at Ra and noticed that she hadn't a lot left in her glass.

"Would you like a top up?"

Ra picked up her glass and finished what was left quickly.

"I'll pay but would you get them the bar staff probably know you better than me so I think you will get served a bit quicker."

Millie stood up and smiled. She disappeared into the pub.

"Why are you going to take Henry with you I could look after him for you?

Katy looked straight at Ra, she was upset and hurt.

"I know but I want him to get used to where I am going to work. You don't know how long you are going to stay and I allow him to stay with you all the time when the time comes it will be hard."

The tears were sitting in the corner of her eyes but what Ra was saying was right. A hand reached and touch her arm it felt so warm and comforting. She looked up and smiled.

"Here we go its getting a bit quieter in there so getting served was a bit easier."

 Millie sat down and sipped her rum and coke.

"Have you ever heard from any of your family since you moved down here."

Where did that come from. Was she asking this because she was curious or had she been recognised.

"No nothing."

She wanted to change the subject but would it draw attention. She looked away and sipped her drink.

"Millie its lovely to see you in here, how are you?"

She looked up and grimaced. The figure in front was well different.

"Very well thankyou."

Silence nobody moved, Ra looked at Millie waiting for her to break the silence and continue the conversation. There eyes met and Millie glared.

"How are you haven't seen you in the village for a while?"

"Oh you know how it is with the business travel here travel there. I only came back from Portugal yesterday. Closed another deal."

Ra smirked as she looked at Millie, she could understand why partaking in conversation was the wrong way to go. The atmosphere was cold and difficult but the egotist still didn't seem to get the hint that there time was over and they should go.

Millie finished her drink rather quick and shook her glass at Ra. Ra nodded and Millie excused herself to the bar.

Unfortunately the figure followed her so there was more conversation to come.

Ra looked over at Katy and saw an ashen face. She was very still and staring.

"Are you ok you look like you have seen a ghost?"

She still didn't move.

"Katy?"

"It's her ……………………………………………."

"What do you mean her?"

"The family in my village she's the mother. What's she doing here, how does she know your friend, did she recognise me, if she did I'll have to go move on find somewhere else."

"Hang on a minute there is probably a perfectly reasonable answer so we will ask Millie when she comes back. Don't panic."

Katy sat hugging her glass and staring at the fence in front.

Millie returned with more drinks. She had an extra shot glass on the tray. As soon as she sat the shot glass was empty.

"That woman is a nightmare I wish I had never agreed to allow her daughter onto the course."

"She does seem a little full of herself. I haven't seen her around the village?"

"No she comes from down the coast Turbridge. Her husband has his own business. I think it's something to do with imports and exports. Her daughter is always going on about how she is going take over when her parents retire."

Katy sat still eyes fixed towards the fence. What she was hearing didn't make her feel any safer, she didn't know if she had been recognised.

Henry groaned and stood up. He'd been sitting down for to long and his legs felt like twigs.

Ra placed her hand on the top of his head and smiled.

"Hello handsome don't worry we'll be going soon if that's ok?"

She looked over at Millie who was sipping her beer. She stopped.

"Oh yes that's fine I have to say I have had a lovely evening with you its just a shame she appeared."

The drinks were finished and they made their way out of the beer garden. The village was quiet no noise could be heard from the pub.

Henry trotted on in front sniffing at the air.

" Will you be ok for tomorrow you can come later if you want I don't mind."

"No I should be fine it won't take long to get home."

They reached the crossway and said goodbye.

Ra walked through the gully besides the bakery and joined the road back home.

"Are you going to say anything or do I have to sing to myself?"

She looked to her left to the figure who seemed disinterested in the moonlight bouncing of the trees guiding their way home.

Not a word. Ra shrugged her shoulders and carried on. Henry was marching in front looking for any movement.

"Why was she there. Do you think it's an omen she comes into the pub and speaks to your friend while I am sitting there?"

"I think your worrying over nothing it was just a coincidence."

The journey home was quiet and subdued. Ra unlocked the front door and all piled in. Henry straight to his water bowl and buried his head.

Ra unlocked the back door and looked outside, everything seemed ok. She turned and looked at Katy her face was lost in a situation Ra could not help her with.

"You go of to bed I'll sort Henry out. If you want to talk tomorrow we will."

Katy turned and went. She sighed the bedroom felt safe only her thoughts could worry her. Maybe Ra was right it was just a coincidence.

The night seemed to drag on and Katy felt apprehensive. She listened for any movement in the house but everything seemed quiet. Even though the curtains were closed it was looking like another beautiful day.

She entered the hallway and headed for the bathroom, still no noise.

The bathroom door slowly opened and Katy froze her heart beat increased.

Henry appeared and trotted in.

"Thank god. Morning handsome how are you?"

He sat besides her and looked. What did he want she was sure Ra had given him his breakfast.

Katy walked towards the kitchen but couldn't' hear anything why?

Ra wasn't there, the kettle wasn't bubbling away on the stove. She looked towards the table and there was a note leaning against the roses.

"Morning I hope you had a goodnights sleep. I know I said I was taking Henry with me but thought you made need the company after last night. I only intend to be a few hours so help yourself. Henry's dinner is in the fridge and there's some fresh cooked chicken for you as well."

Katy smiled and looked out the window. Henry was sitting in his favourite spot by the shed watching the birds. She was not alone. She turned and placed the kettle on the stove it had been along time since she was home alone what was she going to do.

"Well good morning handsome."

Henry was stood in the doorway eyes wide tail wagging.

Katy sat at the table to eat her breakfast and Henry sat by her feet. His mouth was leaking water onto the floor waiting for any leftovers.

An hour had passed Katy was still sitting at the table hugging the mug in her hand. She had all day to do what ever she wanted but didn't feel like doing anything. Henry was lying on the floor he hadn't shown any signs of wanting to go out but she didn't know what he was used to.

Katy got up and walked around the house she was looking for something to clean or tidy up, nothing there was nothing to do the house was tidy in fact it was more than tidy it was spotless.

Outside was sunny a good day to take Henry out but she would have to be careful where she went. Seeing the mother last night scared her was she recognised would someone come looking for her.

Now she was being stupid, someone looking for her why what had she done what had she seen?

Ra turned up bang on 10:30am. Her hand began to shake as rang the bell. Why was she shaking it wasn't a stranger she was going to work for it was a new friend.

Before she could answer her own question the door opened.

Millie stood in the doorway her hair was hanging like ivy in different places. It looked like she hadn't slept at all.

"Morning I'm not to early you did say 10:30?"

"Morning I know I look a mess but I was working late last night I thought I would finish of my report on Ellies assignment. She is the daughter of that confounded woman who spoilt our evening last night."

"Why is she coming to see you today?"

"Unfortunately yes about 3pm this afternoon it's a shame she couldn't come this morning you would be able to see what I have to put up with."

Ra smiled and followed her through the corridor.

They went passed a room on the left but she didn't have time look in.

The pictures on the wall seemed mismatched a country seen on one side art deco on the other. They came to the end of the corridor and walked through into well something out of the Victorian age, that's the only way she could describe it.

Millie turned and looked at Ra she could see the puzzled look on her face or was it.

"I know you think its strange but this is my study and as I study things Victorian then it would be best to be surrounded by all things Victorian."

Ra's eyes were drawn to a figure on the table by the window. It was nothing like she had ever seen before. Was it animal, human actually anything.

"It's a voodoo doll. I purchased it some years ago from an old house in London. Its over 150 years old. It was found in a box of voodoo cards."

"What made you buy it not the kind of thing that would take my eye?"

"I was trying to find out some information for one of my students and it was on the site I looked on. I agree not something you would normally buy but I was drawn to it so brought it."

Ra didn't feel comfortable it seemed to watch her or was she just being stupid.

"Come on it won't hurt you let me show you the kitchen."

Millie left the room Ra still stood staring. She shivered as though someone had walked over her grave. She noticed she was on her own turned and rushed towards the door. She turned left and followed the footsteps down the hall.

The kitchen was large and bright. It seemed strange to go from an old Victorian room to a modern kitchen with a microwave and coffee maker in the corner.

"Everything in the kitchen is yours just help yourself.

Now it's going to be a warm day so I've taken my work outside on the patio. I'll make a drink and bring it out. Just go through the door in front of you and turn right I'll be out in minute."

Ra headed towards the door. She was relieved they weren't going in that room today it was going to take a while for her to be comfortable there if ever.

"Wow!"

She looked in front of her. The cherry blossom was full of colour and the forest flame looked amazing. The garden looked beautiful and never ending.

Millie appeared behind her with the tea.

They both sat down and tea was poured.

"Your garden is so beautiful how do you keep it this way?"

"A few of the students who come to me look after it. I'll show you the rest of it after there's more beyond the cherry blossom. I love sitting out here when I have had a stressful day if I'm lucky the fox comes in late of a night to have a nose."

Silence fell as they drank their tea. Ra would be bringing Henry next time he would love to relax out here.

"Ok let me show you what I need you to do. We haven't got much to mark at the moment because the students have just finished one project and starting another. This is when I try to get in front."

Millie reached down into a small box she had beside her and pulled out some folders.

"If you could read through a couple of them for me you will get and idea of what they are studying. Once you have done that we can get on with you typing notes. Are you ok with that?

Ra smiled and nodded she was just happy to have a job, something to do and earn a small wage to keep her head above water.

The first paper she began to read was by Andrew Weyborough. It was difficult to understand what he was studying but it seemed he was trying to find out how a young man had got away with murdering his wife and gained the family home from his widowed mother in law.

She continued to read and finally after 2hours had worked it out.

The wife had been poisoned and the police at the time had got proof it was him. The father of the murdered wife had left the family home to her in his will with the understanding that her mother could live out her days there.

The husband was at the time a highly upstanding banker in London and everything looked rosy.

On March 18th 1886 the husband had won a large contract so decided to go out and celebrate. He was taken to a private gambling club and unfortunately as normal it all went down hill from there. He became addicted and quickly got into debt.

He had some kind of insurance against her where if she died the family home would be turned over to her husband who could then do as he wished including making the mother in law leave. The house was worth a substantial amount and would have cleared his debts and more.

The case took three weeks at trial and somehow the husband managed to obtain witnesses with let's just say colourful backgrounds.

Andrew had got copies of the news paper reports at the time showing the husband as he came out of court.

This was disgraceful money had taken another life and ruined a family surprising that it hadn't changed .

She went to close the folder but noticed a small piece of paper sticking out at the bottom. It was different from the others from a notepad it seemed.

She began to read and was confused it had nothing to do with case she had been reading.

Still haven't found anything out yet but will keep looking.

I know their hiding something just need to dig a bit more.

                        HJT

Who was HJT would Millie know anything about?

She looked at the time it was 12:45pm that was a surprise it had felt like an hour had passed.

She rose from the table and went to find Millie.

She was sitting in that room with papers and folders scattered over the floor.

"I know it looks a mess but this is my organised chaos. How did you get on do you think you'll get to grips with it?"

"I only red one so far but very interesting. I just wanted to ask you, I was reading a paper by Andrew about a murder."

"Oh the wife and home, not a nice one but he got what he deserved in the end. The husband didn't know about another daughter which the father had from another relationship and she found more proof. Even though he couldn't be retried for her murder he was tried for fraud. Got 15 years in prison lasted 6 and died. Serves him right what goes round comes around I've always said."

"Well that's good news. What I wanted to ask is that I found this piece of paper in his folder but it doesn't seem to have anything to do with that case he was studying?"

She handed over the paper. Millie looked puzzled but said nothing.

"I'm seeing him tomorrow I'll ask him. Actually no you can ask him he'll be here at 11:00. Did you find anything in his paper that could do with changing?"

"Just a few spelling issues which I have highlighted but nothing else."

"Well its time for lunch do you want to join me or get off home that handsome chap of yours?"

"I'll go if you don't mind I haven't left Henry alone for this long before."

"Ok c u tomorrow then same time?"

Ra nodded and left.

It was a [8]lovely warm day again but with a gentle breeze to ease the heat. She passed a few walkers in the village as she headed home. The rest of her journey was peaceful.

She came up the path expecting to hear Henry but nothing. Panic began to fill her she wasn't used to coming home to an empty place. She opened the door and nothing. She rushed into the kitchen the back door was locked. There was nobody home. Where had they gone had Katy run of with him, had they had an accident, had they been kidnapped.

"You daft fool stop it now Katy has just taken him out for a walk it's a lovely day and probably boring being at home on your own in a strange place."

Ra went over to the fridge and pulled out a cold jug full of home made lemonade. She took a sip and sighed it was very refreshing. She walked over to the bread bin two lovely cobs were still there.

"Ham salad sounds lovely."

She poured herself another glass of lemonade and placed it on her tray.

Even though it was lovely and warm outside and her cobs were full of flavour she wasn't enjoying it.

Henry should be sitting in front of her dribbling waiting for his little treat.

"I hope he's having a good time?"

It didn't make her feel any better. How can she feel so low it wasn't as though he was never coming back. He probably didn't even miss her.

She looked out of the window and nothing, no dog or human making their way up the path. It was still light and seemed warm but her heart was beginning to pound was he ok was Katy ok, were they lost or in trouble.

These thoughts going through her mind weren't helping.

The time was now 7.35pm she hadn't been apart from Henry for this long ever. It hurt!

4

Henry started to whine

"Ok I know we have seen enough for today. Lets go Ra will kill me for keeping you out for so long but she'll understand when I tell her what we have seen going on.

They turned and started walking back up the path that seemed to just appear.

The sun was still out but starting to drop, the clouds looked as though they were wrapping themselves around it ready for the night.

"I don't think its far to go now Henry I can remember seeing that house on our way down."

Henry looked up and wagged his tail.

"I wonder if Ra has ever been down this way its been a lovely peaceful walk. Actually we haven't seen anyone all day. Not sure if that is a good or a bad thing. I would like to come back down here again though I have a feeling that there is another path behind those bushes."

Henry suddenly stopped and began to huff.

"What's the matter Henry its just a rabbit in the bush look you see its ears."

Henry moved slowly towards the bush and then jumped at the rabbit. His paws slammed onto the ground but no rabbit.

He looked up at Katy and wagged his tail.

"I think you missed it fella come on lets go."

Of they went enjoying the final bit of sun left.

"Yeah here we are go on Henry go find mommy."

Henry began barking and ran of up the drive. Before he got to the door it flung open and Ra appeared arms outstretched and smiling from ear to ear.

"Hello handsome where have you been I have so missed you both."

Katy stopped and looked she felt a tear well up in her eye nobody had ever said that before.

Ra looked up and smiled.

"Kettles on come on tell me what you've been doing all day."

They all disappeared into the house.

Henry went straight to his bowl and began to drink the fresh cold water.

"So where did you go today then? "

"To be honest I'm not quite sure. We just kept walking towards the beach then came across a hidden path. Well it wasn't hidden just covered with ivy. Henry went through first so of course I had to follow.

Ra looked up at her and smiled. She knew it was an excuse but she would have done the same.

The teapot jangled as Ra put the lid on. It was an old teapot but Ra loved it and always felt the tea tasted better.

Henry lay down by the kitchen table where the floor was nice and cold. He gave a big groan and placed his head on the tiled floor.

"You seemed to have tired him out. I hope he'll be ok for tomorrow. "

"Why what is happening tomorrow? "

Millie is having a few of her students over tomorrow to have their course work assessed. I don't know why she's not doing it at the university. "

Katy seemed to go a little quiet but then seemed to snap out of it.

"Now come on Katy tell me all about today"

Katy started from the beginning and described in detail what she had seen and that the trail they had been on went a lot further. She hinted to Ra that it would be nice for them all to walk along it another day and find out where it leads to.

Ra had got the fire going in the living room and they both began to sink into the chairs watching the flames attempting a Mexican wave.

The room was quiet and the air was warm. Henry was twitching as he slept. Ra opened her eyes and looked at the clock.

Ra stood up and went over to Katy who was sound asleep.

"Katy Katy come on I think it's time we went to bed. "

Katy sat up and rubbed the top of her head. She smiled as she looked at the figure in front of her.

"How long have I been a asleep ? "

"We've been asleep for at least an hour, I've only just woke up. I would have left you here but you started to talk. "

Katy looked shocked had she said something she shouldn't have.

"Don't worry you didn't embarrass yourself now of you go I'll get the cups out. "

Katy stood up and disappeared into the hallway.

Ra took the cups to the sink then opened the backdoor for Henry.

"Round Hay Ruby. I wonder what she meant. "

Henry came trotting back in and went of to bed.

Ra slid under the bed clothes and lay looking at the ceiling. Was that name a place, an object, a person. She couldn't fathom out what but it was such a strange thing to mumble in your sleep.

5

Ra woke to Henry sitting starring at her.

"Well good Morning handsome what can I do for you?

Henry stood up wagged his tail and disappeared out the door. She could hear a noise coming from the kitchen.

She walked down the hallway and began to smell bacon.

"Morning take a seat and I'll bring the teapot over. "

Katy was stood over the stove turning the bacon in the frying pan. Ray sat at the table and poured the tea.

"I thought I'd cook you a hearty breakfast just in case your late. At least I know you've had one good meal. "

Ra looked over at the stove and smiled.

Within 10 minutes they were both tucking into breakfast.

Henry sat by the table patiently waiting. The food smelt good and he knew he would get some.

Katy looked down at him and rubbed his head.

" I haven't forgotten you. "

She went over to the work top and picked up his bowl.

By now Henry was doing his impression of a prancing horse. His head was in his bowl before she could put it on the floor.

After a short while the plates were empty and they both sat at the table clutching there cups of tea.

"Thankyou for that it was lovely. I don't think I will need any lunch. "

Katy smiled and looked outside.

"It looks like it's going to be a lovely day again today. "

Ra nodded then looked at the clock.

"Come on Henry let's get ready. He jumped up and trotted of down the hallway.

Ra picked up her bag and placed it over her head.

"Were going now see you later. "

Ra looked back towards the kitchen but heard nothing.

She slipped Henry's collar on and opened the door.

"Bye have a good day. "

The front door closed and they were gone.

Ra headed down the drive then stopped.

"Come on Henry let's go this way we have time. "

Henry ran on ahead sniffing the ground as he went.

The path seemed to get wider as they walked along it.

The sun was moving across the sky getting brighter as it went.

Ra came to the end of the path and down to Henry.

"Well that was a nice change and it seemed quicker as well. Come on Millie's house is just there. "

Henry wagged his tail and walked on. Ra walked up the path and went to knock on the door as it swung open. Ra jumped backwards and Henry gave out a deep bark.

"Morning didn't expect to see you there you normally come around the back. "

"We would normally but I've found a shortcut and it was such a lovely walk to. Great way to start the day. "

Millie went to the postbox and took out the contents.

Henry had already disappeared into the house. Millie and Ra headed for the kitchen.

I've already made the tea and I presume his lord and master will want his biscuits. "

As expected Henry was sitting by cupboard waiting for his biscuits.

"Ok I'm coming. "

Ra grabbed a handful of biscuits and placed them in the floor.

Henry nudged a few out of the way and grabbed a marrowbone.

Millie sat at the table while Ra brought the teapot and cups over.

"You know I don't know why we bother having lost its either bills or promotion leaflets for god knows what. You see look at this as if I'm interested in anything like that. "

Ra took the leaflet and began to read it. She looked over at Millie and smiled.

"Do you think it's funny? Fancy sending me something like that I'm an upstanding pillar of the community. Cheek. "

"Well quite a few people do use dating agency's these days. But I can see that they have made a mistake in this instance. Do you think it was meant for your neighbour? "

Millie looked up and began to giggle. "I wouldn't have thought so. My neighbour is 87 in a wheelchair and rumour is that he's o' incontinent to. "

Ra looked at her as the room erupted into laughter.

Half an hour past and they were still tittering.

"Come on we'd better get started that Andrew will be round to speak about his course work. You can deal with that it will be good practise. "

Ra looked at the clock she still had plenty of time to get prepared.

Millie walked of into the study and Ra followed by Henry went into the living room. Ra sat and looked out of the window. The sun was fighting its way through the maze of flowers leaving reflective patterns on the carpet.

She opened the folder in front of her and began to scan through the pages highlighting any errors she spotted.

Henry was lying by the window taking in the sun. His ears suddenly pricked up and he sat up. He began to huff.

"What's the matter handsome is there something out there? "

Ra looked at the time it was nearly 11am. She got out of the chair and headed down the hallway to the front door.

The pebbles on the path began crunch. Henry began to bark.

The doorbell rang as Ra began to open the door. Henry dived out at the figure standing there. He began to sniffed around the person standing there.

"Hi I've come to see Miss Gentry about my course work. "

The voice was broken and quiet.

"Morning my names Ra I'm Miss Ventry's assistant and this is Henry. If you'll just follow me we will go into the living room. "

Ray turned and disappeared down the hallway. She walked halfway down the hallway and then stopped. There was no student or Henry. When she looked they were both still standing on the doorstep.

"Come on Henry we have work to do. "

Henry came trotting down the hallway followed by an off balance scruffy individual who would have gone flying if he hadn't caught hold of the door handle.

"You must be Andrew? " Ra held out her hand.

He rubbed his hands down the front of his trousers and grabbed her hand. His grip was gentle but his hand was sweaty.

"Take a seat and I'll go and get Miss Ventry. "

"Is the dog staying in here? "

Ra turned and looked "I won't be long you'll be fine. "

He looked at the dog as Ra left the room.

She left the room and headed into the study.

"Millie that Andrews here do you want to speak to him? "

Millie looked up from the papers on her desk, her glasses were just balancing on the bottom of her nose.

" I suppose I better had he has made the effort to come here. "

They both walked down the hallway. Footsteps in sync. It probably sounded like the firing squad marching to their next victim.

They entered the room and Andrew hadn't moved an inch since Ra had left the room.

"Morning Andrew thankyou for coming over to see me I really appreciate it. Now your previous assignment I have passed it on to Ra my assistant to mark as I have so much work to mark. She is very good and will go through everything with you. "

She looked at Ra and smiled.

Ra turned and looked at Andrew. She was not expecting that.

"Ok can I get you a drink before we get started? "

"Yes please could I have some water? "

Ra headed into the kitchen this time followed by Henry.

"I can't understand why he's so nervous. It doesn't seem just you there's something more. "

Henry sat tilting his head trying to show he understood.

Of they went back down the hallway into a very quiet room.

Andrew took the glass of Ra and placed it on the table next to him.

"Ok let's get started then. I have looked through your assignment and have to say it was very in depth. It must have taken along time to collect the evidence. What made you decide to look into that crime ? "

"Well Miss Ventry asked the class to look into a crime which had occurred in the Victorian times that hadn't made the front pages. It took me about a month to come across this story but when I began to read it I couldn't out it down. "

"Your evidence is very explicit. I do have one question though what does HJT mean? "

Andrew looked puzzled then he had a light bulb moment and smiled.

"The piece of paper I found. No I'm still trying to find out. I do know it's nothing to do with the crime I investigated. I think someone else must have been reading the book I found it in. I am determined to find out though. You never know if they started looking into a new investigation. I wouldn't mind taking a look at it. "

"Well have you got anymore assignments? "

"I don't think so I would have to ask. "

"Let me go and ask her while your here. "

Henry looked up and then over at Andrew. Should he stay and watch or follow his mom.

He decided to sit and watch the figure curling up on the chair.

Ra entered the study and looked over at the desk. There was no movement could she be asleep.

She walked over to the desk and leaned towards Millie's left ear.

"I'm not asleep just thinking. "

Ra stepped back and sighed.

"Andrew would like to know if you have another assignment for him? "

Millie turned and looked up at Ra her glasses were leaning to the left of her face and you could see a slight dent in her skin where she had been leaning on them.

" No that was the only assignment he had to do. He can use what time he has left to do what he wants. But if he does do something else you will have to tell him it won't go to his final marks at the end of term. "

"I don't think he minds. Do you know that piece of paper he found with the letters on, he seems to want to look into that more. "

Millie turned back to her desk and picked up some notes.

Ra was about to leave then stopped.

"Millie would you mind if I helped him look into this note I find it intriguing to and want to know more about it? "

"No that's ok as long as your still able to help me. "

"Oh that goes without saying. "

Ra smiled and disappeared into the hallway.

Andrew had managed to pull himself out of the chair and was standing by the window.

"She said that's fine but she won't be able to mark it though. "

Andrew looked and smiled.

"I do have an idea though if you agree? "

He turned and looked.

"I would like to help you if I can it is interesting. Anyway two heads are better than one and look at all the information you have to hand here. Millie has plenty of newspaper cuttings from years gone by and you'll be able to dip into her knowledge. Now how good does that sound? "

Andrew raised his eyebrows she was talking sense. Without being able to come here and also an extra pair of eyes it would take him forever and he would eventually give up.

"Ok if does sound a very good proposition I will be happy to accept. "

Ra shot a glare of surprise at him. The cheek of it he will accept. Really he would have no choice.

" If you want come here say Thursday. That will give me time to catch up and you chance to start getting some information together. "

Andrew nodded and picked up his rucksack. They both headed towards the door followed by Henry.

"I'll see you Thursday same time? "

Ra nodded and began to close the door.

There weren't many books but it wouldn't be a cottage without some. Katy looked some were big some looked and sounded boring.

She sighed "I didn't think it was this difficult to choose a book. "

She carried on looking and stopped at a book that seemed to be asking he for to take it. She pulled the edge of the book and turned the cover to face her.

The Princess Clipper.

She turned the book over and then went and sat on the chair by the window. The sun was high and you could feel the warmth on the chair as she sat down.

Something moved in the garden and Katy looked up. She looked over at the clock and it was 3:15pm. She was surprised and wondered how long she had been sitting there. She looked at the page there was only a few lines left to read and she would be on chapter 4.

The book was only a few hundred pages but as she was reading it some of it sounded familiar. The places it described the times. But why she didn't know.

She carried herself a hot cup of tea back to the chair picked up the book and carried on. She got to chapter 6 and decided to put it away for the day.

" Ra should be back soon better get the kettle on. "

She placed the book on the table and headed for the kitchen.

The back door was open and the smell of fresh lavender was finding it's way into the kitchen. She breathed in the fresh smell as she heard the front door open.

Roo,Roo,Roo. Henry came charging down the hallway like a dog possessed.

Katy turned and bent down. "Well hello handsome and what kind of day have you had? "

He skidded the last few inches straight into Katy's arms pushing her over as he did.

Ra followed only to be met by a mix of legs in the air and laughter.

" I think he's happy to see you. Are you ok? "

Katy looked up at Ra and managed to raise her left arm in acknowledgement before Henry buried his head in her chest.

"Well while you two are playing I'll put the kettle on. "

Ra stepped over the mound on the kitchen floor and headed for the sink.

"Ok that's enough Henry let's go get some food from the garden. "

Henry jumped up and shot out into the garden barking as he went.

"Well someone seems to have had a good day? "

Ra looked over at Katy.

"He was on guard duty. One of Millie 's students came over to have his assignment marked and Henry thought it was his duty to watch every move he made. It was quite funny actually. Every time Henry moved he seemed to crumple further into the chair. "

Katy placed the teapot on the table as Ra was putting Henry's food in his bowl.

"Henry dinner. "

Ra began to tell Katy about how she was going to help Andrew look into the piece of paper he had found in the book.

"That sounds interesting I wonder what you will find? "

They carried on chatting and deciding what to have to eat. Eventually meat and mash was decided. Within 90 minutes they were sitting at the table tucking into it. Henry sat in his usual place dribbling.

Cutlery clanked on the table and empty plates shuffled. Both had enjoyed the food and could have eaten more.

"That was scrumptious I could eat again. "

Ra smiled and headed for the kitchen with the empty plates.

By 7:45 the crocks were put away and they were both sitting in the living room watching tv.

Katy looked over at the bookshelf feeling tempted to carry on reading but her eyes wouldn't cope.

Ra looked at the clock. It was only 8:45pm but she was tired.

"Well I don't know about you but I'm of to bed. I need match sticks to keep my eyes open. "

Katy smiled and picked up the empty cups of the table.

Ra headed to the back door followed by Henry.

"Come on handsome of you go. "

Henry trotted out and stood on the grass sniffing the air.

Katy was undressed and in bed by the time Ra came down the hallway. She went to close the curtains and looked down the path at the moon shining on the road. The silhouette of a fox appeared as it sniffed about. Katy smiled and watched until it dissappeared.

She lay there trying to go to sleep but the book kept creeping into her head. Why it was only another book, what was so special about this one.

She sat up on the edge of the bed and looked through the opening she had left in the curtains. The fox had come back and was sniffing along the path. Suddenly she spotted movement in the hedge and her heart began to pound. Out dived two fox cubs jumping on each other.

Katy gave out a deep sigh and rolled back into bed. Hopefully she would be able to get some sleep.

A gap appeared by the door and Katy shot up. "Hello*

The door slowly opened and Ra walked in with a tray.

"Morning, you seemed to have been tossing about quite a bit in the night so I thought I would let you sleep in a bit longer.

"What time is it? "

"Only 9:30am. I don't have to be at Millie's until 11am so there's no rush. "

Ra placed the tray on the side and left.

Katy sniffed at the tray. It was only toast and marmalade but smelt so good.

She sat on the edge of the bed and munched away.

An hour later she appeared in the kitchen. It was all quiet. Ra and Henry had already gone.

It looked like it was going to be another lovely day but she didn't feel like going walking.

She got herself a glass of water and headed into the living room towards the bookshelf.

The sun hadn't appeared yet but you could see it hiding behind the clouds but as the day went on she knew it would be lovely and warm in the chair.

She flipped through the pages to find out where she had got to.

" The boat was sinking and there was nobody around to help. Her legs were beginning to feel numb and she was getting tired. "

"That must be very interesting? "

Katy screamed and leapt up out of the chair followed by the book. Henry jumped back and barked. Katy turned in mid flight to see Ra standing at the kitchen door.

"I'm sorry I didn't mean to startle you. You looked so enthralled in that book I didn't want to disturb you.

Katy took a deep breath and headed towards the kitchen.

"How long were you standing there for? "

"About 5minutes. Tea? "

Katy nodded and went and sat at the table.

Ra placed the cups on the table and sat opposite.

"What book are you reading anyway? "

"it's called The Princess Clipper. It tells you of the journeys it made. The funny thing is I feel I have red it before but not sure where or when. "

"Now that is strange. Come on let's take this tea into the living room.

They both disappeared and slipped into the chairs by the window.

"How is your student getting on? "

" Well he's finished his assignment but asked to do another project. He wants to look into a note he found in one of the books. He's hoping it will head to something interesting. I said I would help. "

Katy tried to look interested as she listened but her mind was elsewhere.

Henry came in from the kitchen and placed himself besides Ra. She reached over and placed her hand on top of his head. It felt lovely and warm.

"How is he going to work that out? "

"Well I said we should go to the bookshop in the village and see if they no anything about it. "

Ra looked over to where Katy was sitting. She was staring out of the window.

"Are you ok? "

Nothing. Ra called her name again and finally she turned to look.

" Hello are you ok? "

Katy smiled.

"Have you ever picked up a book and once started you can't out it down? "

"There has been the odd one. "

"This book is not really the kind of book I would normally read. When I'm reading it I feel know or have been to some of the areas it describes. "

"Maybe you have red it before. "

Katy looked but didn't seem convinced.

Ra could see the look of concern in her face.

"How do you fancy a walk into the village. Stretch your legs? "

She didn't feel like it but sitting in the house all day wouldn't do her any good.

Henry was standing by the front waiting for his collar.

Ra closed the front door and locked it.

The walk to the village was quiet but it was still warm.

"The pub is just round the corner let's have a drink.

Katy looked a little nervous but followed willingly.

They walked into the garden and headed for the table by the rose bush.

"What would you like to drink? "

"Could I have a shandy please? "

Ra went into the pub leaving Katy with Henry.

She reached over and rubbed his head. He groaned and looked up.

"I have missed you today. Do you think your mom would let me take you a hike tomorrow. I wouldn't mind looking for that path again and see where it goes. Henry looked up and wagged his tail.

Ra came back with a tray. 2 drinks, crisps, nuts and a bowl of water for Henry.

"There we go not sure if you would like crisps or nuts so I got both. "

Katy smiled and picked up her drink. It was cold and refreshing. She gave out a sign and smiled.

" I thought this would do us good instead of being stuck in the house all the time.

The air was warm and the rose bush oozed aroma.

Ra looked over at Katy and down at Henry. It was times like this that made her happy she had moved here.

Another couple came through the gate and sat at the table behind them. Henry lifted his head and then lay back down.

"Would you like a nut? "

The question didn't register. Katy was looking over towards the fence.

Ra reached over and touched her arm. Katy turned round looking shocked. Ra held out the packet of nuts.

Katy shook her head and sipped her drink.

7

The curtains began to wave with a gentle breeze from the open window.

She gave a big sigh and rolled over. Eyes finally wide open she was awake.

The house was quiet so it must be after 9:30 am. So much for going out with Henry.

By the time she had made her way into the kitchen got her tea and toast then planted herself in the chair by the window it was 10:48am.

She looked out the window but the garden was still.

She picked the book of the shelf and was gone back into the life of the Princess Clipper.

The breeze outside was gentle but warm. Her heart was pumping with anxiety, why didn't they help her she had nowhere to go. The rocks were to dangerous and the path she took to the beach was where the barrels were being loaded.

She placed the book on her lap and took a deep breath. She felt as though she was there standing right next to her. What should she do. What could she do. Why did they not help her, what was so important.

She stood up and stretched. A cup of tea was called for.

Half an hour later she was sitting outside ready to take on the next chapter.

"Roo,Roo,Roo. "

Henry shot through the door tail rotating jumping with excitement. He sat in front of Katy waiting for that head rub but nothing. She was still fighting her battle.

Henry placed his paw on her knee.

"Hello handsome where did you come from, have you had a good day? "

"Hi would you like a tea? "

Katy lifted her cup and nodded that one had gone cold.

Henry still sat waiting for his head rub.

"Here you go nice and hot. "

Ra sat andsignehd as she took a sip.

"How was your day anything interesting? "

"Well Andrew went of into the village yesterday to the book shop. He spoke to the owner about the note he had found. They weren't sure what it meant but told him to go and speak to a villager who had lived here for years. So we went and spoke to him today. He seems to think the three letters could have something to do with harbour records in the next village. "

"How's the book? "

"I think I'm halfway through. The more I read it though the more I feel I'm becoming her. I feel her heart beat when she panics or feel the heat from the sun when she stands on the beach. It's really weird. " I've never felt like this when I've red a book before. "

She looked over at Ra for and answer.

"Well it seems to have got under your skin. "

"What do you mean? "

" Wells it's woken something in the back of your mind. You said the book looked familiar, maybe you had seen it somewhere before. "

"I was never much of a reader when I lived at home and we didn't have those kind of books in the house. "

Ra looked up and smiled. This was something she could not answer.

Katy looked at the book. Why was it so familiar where had she seen it before.

"Do you want to help me get these leaves up before they become a carpet? "

Katy nodded and headed for the back door followed by Henry and Ra.

The sun began to hide behind the clouds as they scraped the leaves into large piles. Henry lay in the middle of the lawn sniffing the air.

Ra stud up straight stretching her back. "There we go all one nice pile. "

She headed back towards the small shed in the corner.

"Wee woohoo catch it. "

Ra turned and looked. The leaves were no longer in a nice tidy pile. Katy was jumping into the pile throwing leaves in the air as Henry was running head down through the pile.

Ra stood and stared. The stern look on her face gave way to smile. It was lovely to hear and see such joy and laughter she felt like crying.

Within in a few minutes Katy and Henry were slumped on the grass surrounded by leaves.

Katy looked over at Ra and smiled.

"Sorry I couldn't resist it. I think Henry enjoyed himself? "

They both looked over to see him sprawled out on the grass legs in the air.

Ra disappeared into the kitchen and came out with drinks and a chew for Henry only to find both fast asleep.

She sat on the patio and took a deep breath.

Half an hour passed and both were still asleep. You could feel the night air coming in. Ra went over to Katy and gave her a nudge.

"Come on its best we go in its starting to get chilly. "

Katy looked up and began to push herself up of the grass. "We've got to get these leaves up. "

"Don't worry we can do it another day. "

Henry stirred and groaned as he sat up.

They all disappeared into the sitting room

Ra switched on the tv to see what had been going on in the world. By the time she sat down both were asleep. Henry in his bed snoring away and Katy in the chair next to the window.

Ra waited half an hour then gave Katy a nudge.

"Come on I think you should go to bed. "

Katy turned and looked. without a word she smiled and went up the hallway.

The morning was dry but no sun. Henry was fast asleep in his bed and there was no noise coming from Katy's room.

It was peaceful and serene. Times like these she felt very lucky to have the kind of life she had found.

She sensed there was movement coming from the hallway.

A pair of black paws appeared.

"Well good morning glad you could join me. Henry made his way into the kitchen sitting in front of Ra.

"Do you want your biscuits? " Henry wagged his tail looking up to Ra.

She placed a handful in his bowl. He began to inspect what was in there deciding which one to eat first.

She sat back down wrapping her hands around her cup.

Katy was still in bed. Ra looked up at the clock.

"Come handsome time to go. "

Ra picked up her bag and headed down the hallway. She stopped outside Katy's room. There was not a single sound. She smiled and carried on to the front door.

Henry shot of down the drive as she locked the door. She didn't like leaving Katy without saying goodbye but today was different.

Off they marched down the path to the side of the cottage.

Henry sniffing in every bush he passed as Ra looked up to the sky.

15 minutes later they were at Millie's front door.

As she opened the door she could hear voices coming from the dining room. Ra frowned Millie never had visitors this time of the morning.

Henry trotted on ahead and turned into the dining room.

"Well good morning handsome how are you today? "

Ra followed turning into the room. There was Andrew sitting in the chair.

"Morning I hope you didn't mind me coming in early? I have found some more information I wanted to talk to you about. "

Ra stood for a few seconds not knowing what to say. She smiled and then sat opposite.

"I'll get you some tea and take this cheeky chappie outside. Millie stood up and rubbed Henry's head.

"Come on you lets go and look in the garden. "

Both went out the door. Ra moved her bag to the side of the chair and looked at Andrew waiting for him to enlighten he"Ok what have you got? "

"Well you know the book shop owner he called me to say he had some information. I went over yesterday and he gave me these 3 books. He said there were bits of information in them about a girl that had gone missing. He thinks the note may have something to do with that. "

Ra could hear the jangling of a tray coming down the hallway.

"Here we go nice and hot. Henry is still outside deciding if the butterfly flapping around the Wisteria is worth grabbing or not. If you need anything else Im in the study. "

Millie turned and disappeared.

Ra poured the tea as Andrew looked through the books.

"Ok what do we have then? "

"Well what I can gather is the girl was from a well known family in the next village. They had a boat which they used to transport goods around the coast. "

"Was there a boating accident of any kind? "

"Not that I can find. It mainly described how the family were made up of a mother, father, daughter and 2 sons. The sons were the ones who mainly worked with their father on the boat. The daughter would go with them every now and then. "

"Were there any rivalries with other local crews? "

"There probably was but nothing to cause any trouble. "

Andrew looked over at Ra as she drank her tea.

"We could do with finding out the name of the boat. Let's ask Millie if she has anything in her library. "

They both walked down the hallway and into the library. Millie was sitting at her desk looking through a pile of papers.

She hadn't noticed they had entered the room.

"Millie could we pick your brains? "

Millie grunted but didn't move. Ra looked at Andrew then back at Millie.

" You've lived in the village most of your life?

Millie turned "Except for the time I spent in London training. Why what can I help you with? "

"Do you know anything about a family in the next village who used their boat to transport goods around the coast? "

Millie smiled. "You mean the Paiges. I know a little about them. Is that what your investigating, good luck. "

Andrew frowned. "Why do you say that? "

"There have been a few investigations into their daughters disappearance over the years and all have come to a dead end. Nobody has ever explained why. Maybe it's meant to stay unknown. "

Ra sat down facing Millie. "Well would you mind if we pick your brains anyway? "

Millie nodded.

All 3 and Henry sat comparing ideas and asking questions.

It was 6pm when Ra walked through the door. Katy appeared from the kitchen making her way down the hall.

"Are you ok has something happened? "

Ra looked and continued into the kitchen.

Katy followed behind. "I was worried something had happened to you or Henry. You've never been this late. "

Ra turned. "I'm sorry we got talking about this note were looking into and forgot the time. "

Katy gave a sigh of relief and headed for the dining room.

Henry went and lay down on his bed and Ra walked over to the sideboard. She half filled 2 small glasses with whisky.

"Here drink this it will calm your nerves. "

Katy took a small sip and gave out a sharp cough.

"Sorry is it to strong for you? "

Katy took a deep breath and had another sip. This time she didn't cough. It made her throat and tummy feel warm. She looked up at Ra smiled and then shook her head.

Katy walked into the kitchen slowly. Her eyes were half open.

Ra smiled "I think you may be a little tipsy. "

Katy looked over and bobbed out her tongue.

"Come on let's get you to bed. "

All went down the hallway. Ra watched Katy as she went into her room.

She looked down at Henry and smiled.

8

Katy appeared at the kitchen door eyes half open hair looking like a bush.

Ra smiled. "Head feeling a bit heavy? "

"It feels like a hundred drums banging at the same time and my mouth tastes of rubbish. "

She sat at the table and lay her head on the table.

"Here drink this it will help. "

Katy took a sip and cringed.

"Okay I'm of I shouldn't be to late. At least you have Henry today. "

Katy looked over at Henry and smiled. Lots of cuddles to keep her warm.

Ra bent down and rubbed his head. Henry's tail began to slow. She was leaving him.

He followed her down the hall and watched the door close.

He dropped his head for a second then seemed to remember that Katy was still there. Head up he turned and trotted back into the kitchen. Katy wasn't there. He turned and found her sitting in the chair by the window. He plonked himself down beside her and groaned. Katy's hand dropped over the side of the chair and she began to massage his head.

"Oh I do hope this headache goes soon. Don't feel like reading and walking is to much effort. "

She looked at her cup and headed for the kitchen. Another coffee was needed. She sat back down in the chair and held her cup to her chin.

Ra and Andrew were sat in the study reading through are large pile of books Millie had got out for them.

"Here's something. " Ra moved closer to Andrew and pointed to a paragraph.

"It says that around the time the girl disappeared there was a lot of smuggling going on. They believe some of the locals were involved. "

"Does it mention any names of if they had anybody under suspicion? "

Ra finished the page then looked at the wall.

" I bet if we go to the library in town we should be able to find out more. How do you fancy a trip tomorrow? "

"Sounds a good idea to me. "

Millie came in with to hot mugs of tea.

" How are we getting on? "

"We've found some information but think it's a good idea to go to the library in town tomorrow to find out more. "

Millie smiled. "I'm not sure but there used to be an old colleague of mine worked in the history section. Leave it with me. I'll make some calls and let you know in the morning. "

Ra and Andrew smiled then carried on looking through the books.

Ra looked up at the clock and then rubbed her eyes.

"I think we've done enough today. Do you want to meet here at 8:30 tomorrow morning? "

Andrew nodded and put some books in his rucksack.

"I'll have a read through these tonight. "

Both stood and stretched. Andrew headed to the front door as Ra went to the kitchen.

"Were meeting here at 8:30 in the morning is that ok? "

Millie turned and smiled.

It seemed strange walking home without Henry even though she had done it before.

The evenings were starting to close in Ra thought it may be a good idea to start walking home through the village.

She was not far from home but suddenly began to feel nervous as though there was something or someone watching her. She kept her walking pace the same but pulled her bag closer to her body. The path was coming to an end and she would be back on the road.

As she got to the road she stopped and took a deep breath, there was a car parked at the bottom of the path towards the cottage. There were 2 people sitting in the front. Who were they, what did they want. Were they something to do with her husband. Had he found her after all this time. But why would he look for her now?

She walked passed the car and looked. The driver smiled and tipped his head forward. She didn't recognise him. She carried on heart racing wondering what too do.

As she approached the gate she knew they would see her go in. She didn't want to put Katy and Henry in danger so carried on up the hill. As she got to the bend she turned and looked the car had gone. A big deep breath eased out of her mouth.

She walked passed the cottage and continued up the hill. As she approached the bend she turned and looked. The car had definitely gone. She took a deep breath and headed back towards the cottage.

Halfway down the lane she was met by Henry and Katy.

"Are you ok we watched you walk passed the cottage? "

"I'm fine just thought I spotted someone walking up the path. Just being nosey really. Come on let's get the kettle on and have a nice cup of tea. "

Ra turned and looked down the path as they entered the cottage. Nobody there.

By 6:30 they had all eaten and were sitting comfortable in the lounge.

"Are you sure your ok you didn't seem to have much to say at dinner? "

"Well to tell you the truth as I was coming home I spotted a car at the end of the road. There were 2men sitting in it and I didn't recognise them. I was going to ask them if they were lost but felt to nervous. They watched me walk up the lane to the cottage and that's why I carried on up the path. "

Katy looked shocked. "Do you think they were watching you or maybe the cottage? "

"I don't know maybe I'm just being silly. Now who's for tea and biscuits? "

Henry jumped up and headed for the kitchen. A few minutes later Ra appeared with a tray.

"Here we go. "

Ra sat and held her hands around the cup.

"I wouldn't worry they were probably lost and trying to work out the best route. "

Ra turned to Katy and smiled. She was probably right and she was being silly.

They all retired to bed at 10:30 but Ra couldn't sleep. The car was still playing on her mind.

Morning sun shone through the curtain as Ra woke it was 7:15 time to get up.

She disappeared into the bathroom while Katy and Henry were still asleep.

By the time she was dressed and walking down the hallway she could smell cooking from the kitchen.

"I didn't know you were awake. "

"I got up while you were in the bathroom. I'm doing boiled eggs if that's ok? "

"Sounds lovely I'll get the tea. "

Henry was sitting in his favourite place at the head of the table as they both tucked into breakfast.

"I was wondering if you minded me taking Henry out today? "

Ra looked up as she ate. She was a little taken back by the request as she had never been asked before.

"Where you thinking of going? "

"Do you remember when I told you about that opening I found in some rocks going towards a beach. Well I would like to go there and see if it does actually lead to a beach. If it's nice we could all go there and have a picnic. "

Ra looked down at Henry who was doing his favourite impression of a waterfall.

"Well what do you think handsome would you like to go to the beach? "

Henry looked up and huffed. Ra smiled and gave him a piece of toast.

"Well there's your answer. "

Katy smiled and picked a piece of toast for Henry.

Ra left at 8am but looked down the path to see if there was anyone there.

She decided to go the main road today. It as overcast but warm. She began to wonder what information if any Andrew may have found. It was becoming intriguing and she was enjoying the task Millie had given her.

She placed the key in the front door but before she could turn it the door opened.

"Morning your early is everything ok? "

Andrew turned and headed back into the house. Ra went into the front room and Andrew headed to the kitchen.

On the table were a pile of papers so Andrew must have found something.

Andrew appeared. with a tray of tea and biscuits.

"Where's Millie? "

" She had to go into town. She said someone had called to say they had some information she wanted. She said she shouldn't be to long. "

"Oh ok. Well let's get on then. Did you find out anymore from the bookshop owner? "

"Well do you remember what the professor said about the 2 brothers on that night. She said that one of them didn't want to go which was quite unusual. "

Ra looked at him and didn't flinch. Andrew swallowed and then carried on.

"Do you think he knew something was going to happen or could have been a part of it? "

"He could have been but we need to find more evidence. They said the boat went out the same time as usual and the daughter being there wasn't a surprise even though she didn't go that often. Is there anyway we could get records from the shipping office. It would be good if we could find out what cargo they were fetching and where from. "

They both sat for a moment thinking of what to do next.

Ra sat up straight and looked towards the door.

"Millie may have some old entry books in her study. Come on let's have a look. "

They both disappeared into the study.

Millie wasn't very organised when it came to books but they had to start somewhere. Ra went one side of the study and Andrew went to the other.

A few hours had passed and no joy as yet. Andrew looked up at the clock on the table. 12:30.

"I think we should take a break it's 12:30. "

Ra looked over and nodded into the kitchen they went.

10 minutes later they were sat on the patio enjoy the sun.

"Hi I'm back anyone home? "

"There you are. Is the pot still warm I'm longing for a cup of tea? "

"Yes it should be. "

Millie disappeared into the kitchen.

"Did you get what you were after? "

No sound came from the kitchen. Ra shrugged her shoulders and carried on eating.

Millie appeared with her tea and papers in her other hand.

"Yes I did actually. You will be happy. "

Ra and Andrew turned and looked at Millie.

Millie grabbed another chair and sat down.

"This case your looking into seems to have hit a stumbling block. So I thought what if there is any information in the news archives in the main library. I called a colleague of mine a few days ago and told him about the case. Well he called me last night to say he had found something and for me to go and collect it. "

Millie placed the folder on the table.

Ra and Andrew looked at each other.

"Professor have you looked through them? "

"Andrew can you please call me Millie were not in class. No I haven't looked through them. "

"We were looking in your study to see if we could find any log books for the boats leaving the harbour. "

Millie raised her hand and then left them. She reappeared with 3 large books in her arms.

"I only have these. Unfortunately they are dated before and after the incident but you may get an idea of the kind of cargo they moved. "

The patio fell silent as Ra and Andrew looked through books and papers and Millie sat drinking her tea.

9

The weather was dry but overcast. Katy was packing bits of food and water she had put together for her and Henry.

"Ok food, water and map packed. Now let's get your lead and collar. Henry was gone waiting by the door before Katy had picked up the rucksack.

Katy looked at the clock in the kitchen it was 9:15am.She nodded her head and went to the front door. At least they would have plenty of daylight all she had to do is remember the way.

She double checked the front door and dissappeared down the drive.

The sweet smell of the Hyacinths lifted her spirits as she walked through the dense bush catching her arm on a wild rose bush.

Henry sniffed in a hedge and then jumped back. He looked again and then began to bark.

"What's the matter, what's there? "

Katy moved closer to the bush and moved a branch. She looked at Henry and then smiled. She moved back and began to rab the top of Henry's head.

"You've found a little wrens nest but we can't touch it there are babies in there. Come on let's leave them be. "

Of they continued down the hill.

Katy came to a fork in the road and stopped. Now which way did she go before. She shrugged her shoulders and went left.

After what seemed like hours she came to a fallen tree and plonked her rucksack on the thick trunk. Henry came up to her panting and tail wagging.

"Do you want some water I know I do? "

She opened the bottle and tipped it towards Henry's mouth. Once he'd had enough she took her turn and sipped from the flask.

She began to rummage through the rucksack and pulled out an Apple for herself and some biscuits for Henry.

The breeze was gentle but it felt chilly.

"Ok let's carry on and find out where this path goes. "

Henry jumped up and trotted of Katy smiled as he disappeared through bush.

It had only been as short while when she stopped. She looked up at the sky and could just about see the sun breaking through. Hopefully it would still be out when they get out of the forest.

She came to a path that looked familiar. One part went of to the right which seemed overgrown and the other straight on.But where was Henry she couldn't see him anywhere.

"Henry come on lad where are you?"

Katy turned and looked behind her but he was nowhere to be seen.

"Come on Henry we need to carry on."

There was no sound. She began to worry. It was normal for him to disappear but he wouldn't go far and he would always come back to check you were still there.

"Henry come on boy"

"Ruff ruff."

Katy turned to the right. The noise seemed to be coming from behind the bush but she couldn't see.

She walked towards the bush and peered through the broken branches. There seemed to be a path or what looked like it. She pushed her hand into the bush and began to pull it towards oneside. She grabbed the rucksack and crawled through. Henry was barking in the distance but she couldn't see him as yet.

As she carried on down the path she heard a noise that sounded like wind. The path began to merge into some rocks. There was a small gap in front her. At first she wasn't sure if she could get through but she was going to have ago.

Henry's bark was getting closer as she squeezed through the gap.

Finally she was through and it was amazing.

Henry was splashing in the sea as seagulls flew above. The beach was quiet and smelt so relaxing. Katy put her rucksack on the floor took of her shoes and ran of to the sea.

They both jumped around in the sea like little children seeing the sea for the first time.

Finally Katy came out and fell onto the sand rolling on her back. Henry came charging up and shook the water of him splashing Katy. She took a deep breath and closed her eyes.

The gentle breeze ran over her face like a silk scalf and the smell of the sea flowed under her nose like the waves. Life felt so good.

Suddenly the sun seemed to go in. Katy opened her eyes to see a black head starring at her.

"Well hello handsome what can I do for you?"

Henry began to wag his tail.

Katy looked up at the sky. The sun had moved over to the right.

"Come on I think we need to make a move before it starts to get dark. Henry trotted of towards the rocks seeming to understand what she had said.

Katy packed the bottle in the rucksack and placed it over her shoulder. Henry was standing by the rocks looking back towards Katy.

She turned and looked back at the sea.

"I can't wait to tell Ra about this."

She disappeared through the small hole pushing the rucksack in front of her.

Henry was waiting the other side for her tail wagging.

"OK let's get going want to get home before Ra."

They got to the bush full of ivy. Katy stood in front. Henry thought what the heck and went straight through. Katy grabbed the ivy as it fell back. She took a deep breath and pushed her way through. It felt cold the other side but she was in a forest.

She turned and looked but there was no sign of any entrance just a curtain of ivy lying against a bush.

Henry was sniffing his way through the forest. She looked at what little sky she could see through the trees. It was starting to look dull.

Katy began to walk a little faster. She could feel the cold settling in.

The path seemed to widen and the air began to warm up. They came to the cross in the path and turn of to the left.

Within 10minutes they came to the road and started to walk up the path to the cottage. Hopefully they had got back before Ra.

Katy placed the key in the door and turned.

"Hello Ra are you home?"

Henry had trotted of down the hallway to the kitchen straight to his water.

No answer came back so Katy had done it. She disappeared into the kitchen and opened the fridge to see what she could prepare for tea. There was bacon, sausage and some chops. She stood for a minute then grabbed the chops.

She looked down at Henry who was sniffing the air.

"Let's have some chops with boiled potatoes and vegetables.
"

She placed the chops on a baking tray ready to go in the oven then began to prepare the vegetables. 30 minutes later everything was ready and it was only 4 o'clock.

Katy poured herself a glass of squash from the fridge and went outside. Henry was flat out on the grass taking in the sunshine.

"Hello is anyone home?"

Henry dived up and started barking. Katy turned to see Ra standing at the door way.

"Hello I didn't hear you come in. Have you had a good day?"

"Lets say interesting. Were still looking into that case but don't seem to be getting very far. We have some more information from Millie but we think we need yo go to the main library in the town to dig deeper. I think we'll be going tomorrow. "

"Oh so your still determined to find out what happened?"

"Andrew is definitely going to dig deeper. I don't think he'll stop until we solve it. But I have to say I am enjoying it."

Katy placed the chops in the oven and went back to the fridge.

"Would you like some squash while tea is cooking?"

Ra nodded her head as she went outside and sat on the chair Katy brought out the squash and sat in the chair opposite Ra.

"So what did you get up to today?"

Katy began to tell her about the secluded beach and what a wonderful time she had with Henry.

After they had eaten tea Katy carried on about the walk through the forest and how she had found the hidden path.

"I think if the weather is nice this weekend you should come with us you'll love it."

"Well that sounds like a plan."

Katy smiled and wrapped her hands around the hot cup of tea she had just made.

"Well I think I'm going to turn in my brain is a bit frozen after today."

Ra left the living room placed her cup by the sink and headed down the hallway.

Katy was left in the living room on her own. Henry had followed Ra down the hallway.

10

Ra woke next morning just after 7am. She couldn't remember if she was meeting Andrew at 8am or 8:30am.

She washed and dressed quickly so it would give her a little more time to eat breakfast.

Henry was still a sleep in his bed. He seemed to know that Ra wasn't taking him today so he could sleep longer.

The house was still quiet as Ra packed her bag. She looked in on Henry as she left, he was fast.

The air was chilly as she got to Millie 's house but it was early. She knocked the front door and could hear footsteps coming down the hallway. Millie's face appeared.

"Morning Andrew isn't here yet. I've just put the kettle on."

Millie turned and walked back down the hallway followed by Ra.

"I hope Andrew won't be long I've arranged a meeting for you at the library with an old colleague of mine. I told him of your investigation and he said he has got information that would help."

Ra looked intrigued.

"Morning anyone home?"

Andrew came walking into the kitchen.

"Good morning how are we?"

"Were going to see a man about a boat."

Andrew looked at Ra then over at Millie.

"Here you've just got time to drink this. I've booked an appointment at the library to see a friend of mine. He has a lot of knowledge reference the local shipping industry. He's going to have a look to see what he can find out for you."

Ra looked up at the clock above the cupboards.

"What time is the next bus from the village?"

"Your OK they only run every hour. So it will be 9:30."

Ra looked over at Andrew who was sipping away at his tea.

They both left Millie's house just after 9am. It was only a 10minute walk into the village so there was no need to rush. There were a few people waiting at the bus stop but there would still be plenty of room for them.

The bus slowly eased around the corner and came to stop. They let the passengers on in front of them.

"Morning could I get two adult returns from town please?"

The driver tapped away at the screen.

"That will be £5.80 please."

Ra handed him a £10 note and the driver returned the change.

They both walked of towards the back and took their seats before the bus pulled away.

Neither of them seemed quite chatty which was strange being as though they were investigating an old murder/disappearance.

The streets seemed to get busy so the couldn't be far from the town. The bus turned left and they were on the high street. There was a sign directing you towards the library but there didn't seem yo be a bus stop close by.

"Do you know where we've got get of?"

"I have no idea. I was going to see how close the library was, we've just passed a sign."

The library appeared on the left. Ra pressed the bell so the driver would stop at the next stop for them. Luckily it was only a few hundred yards.

Ra thanked the driver as she got of followed by Andrew.

The pavements were busy with people rushing here and there. Andrew nearly walked into a man who was on his phone but at last minute avoided him.

They walked into the library and were greeted by high elegantly decorated ceilings and cool marble floor.

There was a receptionist sitting at a small table towards the back.

"Morning we have a meeting with Mr Ridge."

"Who shall i say is calling?"

"We are friends if Millie. "

The receptionist looked up and the smiled.

"Mr Ridge I have some people here to see you. They say they are friends of Millie. Ok I'll send them up."

She placed down the phone and looked at them what seemed like for a while before she spoke.

"Ok if you take the stairs to your right, go up to second floor, through the double doors on your left Mr Ridges office is the second door on your left. It has his name on it."

She gave a smile as they disappeared.

A few minutes later they arrived at the door. Ra gave a slight tap and waited.

"Come on in."

The door was heavy and it creaked as she pushed it open.

The man that was sitting behind the desk was small and slim. He raised his head and looked straight at Andrew.

"Hello I believe you know my good friend Millie?"

Ra smiled. "Yes I'm her assistant and this is Andrew one of her students. "

"Now i believe your investigating an old murder?"

Andrew moved closer to the desk.

"Yes that's correct. I found a note in a book and this is where it has led me to. We've come to a bit of a standstill."

Andrew carried on telling him all they had as Ra sat and listened.

"Well I do have quite a few of the logs from the harbour master but it may be difficult to match the entries to the boat your looking for. You see they didn't always put down the owners names if they were locals. I don't suppose you have a description of the family who owned the boat?"

Ra sat up. "Well all we know is that it was mainly a father and his 2 sons but sometimes his daughter would go out with them. We don't have an address for them so I think they must be from the local village."

Andrew looked over and smiled.

"Ok well the 2 closest villages to that harbour were Pennworthing and Brampton. What I can do is contact a few locals to see if they know anything. Here is a list of the logs you can look in and they are in the library downstairs to your left. I will let Millie know when I have some information for you."

"That's great thankyou so much for your help. "

Andrew stood up and reached out his hand. Mr Ridge had a very strong handshake and Andrew cringed under his smile.

They both left the office and headed down the stairs and into the library.

After a few minutes they were both seated on a large wooden table sifting through the log books.

One after another they placed the log books on top of each other.

"This is ridiculous we've only got 2 books left and I haven't found a thing."

Ra looked over at Andrew who was not responding.

He suddenly placed his finger in the middle of the page.

"OK I've found an entry here of a spanish ship called Cessilley. That docked on the same day as 2 local boats were moored. The only thing is they've used initials for the boats not names.

One is TPC and the other is SSL."

"So where does that leave us?"

"Well we know that both boats were there and further down it says the Cessilley left dock at 19:05. SSL left at 19:20 and the TPC left at 18:40."

"So do you think the spanish boat was following the TPC?"

"It seems like it. All we need to do is find a map and see what route they took, but most important we need to find out the name of the boat."

Ra looked up at the large clock on the wall.

"I think we'd better go it's 6:15pm and they close at 7pm."

They picked up the log books and placed them back on the shelves.

The journey back on the bus was quiet. Both were reading the notes they had in front of them

Ra looked out the window to see where they were.

"I think we're nearly there. "

Andrew put his notes in the folder and looked out the window. He recognised one of the cottages before you came into the village.

"OK the next stop is ours."

Ra stood up and pushed the bell button.

A couple got of in front of them and walked round passed the pub.

"Now do you want to meet at Millie's about 9am so we can get a start on these notes we've written?"

Andrew nodded.

"I will see you tomorrow then have a good evening. "

"You to."

Andrew walked towards Millie's house and Ra turned up the side road by the book shop.

Her walk home was quick and quiet.

She opened the door and made her way down the hallway. The kitchen was quiet. She looked to the garden and could see Katy and Henry walking to the far end of the garden.

"Well what are you 2 up to?"

Henry swung round and wagged his tail and Katy turned her head.

"I heard a noise so came out to have a look. Nothing to be seen. It may have been a fox I'm not sure. "

They headed back into the kitchen and started to decide what to have for tea.

"Did you find much out today?"

"I think we did. We spent most of the day at the library taking notes from the ships logs. I'm meeting Andrew earlier tomorrow so we can get ahead. "

"You do know its Saturday and I was going to ask you if you wanted to come to a lovely quiet beach I've found?"

Ra looked and then shook her head.

"I'll have to call Millie and ask her to let Andrew know I will see him on Monday.

11

Ra turned over and grabbed her pillow. She didn't want to get up she was to cosy.

The noise of moving cutlery could be heard from the kitchen. Ra lay in bed for a little while and then jumped out of bed. She couldn't get back to sleep with the noise from the kitchen.

"Morning I hope your hungry I've done us a full breakfast and some sandwiches for our picnic on the beach."

Ra looked at the table. There was toast orange juice and a hot cup of tea.

"Sit yourself down and I'll get the plates out of the oven. Ra sat down and sniffed the air.

Katy placed the hot plate in front of her. It looked as good as it smelt.

Katy placed Henry's bowl on the floor. He dived into it chomping away before Katy sat down.

The kitchen was quiet as they ate. Henry sat by the table waiting for any extras.

" Is the weather going to brighten up today as it looks a little grey out there at the moment?"

Katy turned to Ra standing in the doorway.

"Well I think so. The weather report did say the weather was going to improve. Come on let's get going. You will love the beach I promise."

Henry was waiting at the front door. Katy picked up the rucksack and Ra grabbed Henry's lead.

It didn't seem to take Katy long to find the right path. Henry ran on ahead.

"I hope this cloud breaks by the time we get to the beach."

Katy turned and smiled as they carried on.

"Do you remember how to get there? All I can see ahead is trees and ivy."

"Trust me you will love it. It's just through here."

Ra looked all she could see was ivy.

Katy stepped forward and grabbed some ivy. She pulled it to oneside and went through. Ra stood for a second and followed. The path seemed to grow wider and it felt more open.

"Where's Henry?"

"Don't worry he will be on the beach by now."

They came to the whole in the rock and Katy began to push the rucksack through.

"You will get through but it's a little tight."

Katy carried on through. Ra looked at the hole and sighed. Katy was right it was a tight squeeze. She could smell sea and could hear Henry barking. She pulled herself out of the hole and looked ahead.

"My God this is so beautiful. "

The beach was golden sand and the sea a perfect blue. Katy and Henry were jumping around in the sea. Ra took of her boots and placed them by the rucksack.

"Wait for me."

She ran of down to the sea and jump in the waves. It was cold but felt so refreshing at the same time. Henry decided to chase a crab dipping his head in the water as he tried to grab it.

Katy and Ra began to walk along the beach dragging their feet through the sea. Everything felt so calm and relaxing. Ra felt as though she hadn't got a care in the world.

They walked back to the rucksack and collapsed into the sand while Henry was still trying to catch that dam crab.

Ra and Katy just sat there not a word. The sun had decided to show its face and the warmth felt so good.

Henry finally gave up on the crab and slumped himself down on the sand next to Ra.

Katy lay on the sand and closed her eyes. She wished this moment could last forever.

"Oh look there's a small boat going over to the rocks."

Katy sat up and looked towards the rocks. It was a small sailing boat moving slowly. Her heart began to pump and she could feel butterflies in her stomach. There shouldn't be anyone coming to the beach it was her own small sanctuary.

She jumped and began to put the picnic cutlery in the rucksack.

Ra looked over at her bemused.

"What's wrong why are you packing up?"

"I don't want anyone to see us. If they do they may think this is a public beach.

This is our beach nobody else's. "

Katy turned and headed towards the rock. Within 10minutes they were through the hole and walking towards the ivy bush.

"You can slow down now I don't think anyone can see you from here."

Katy charged on and disappeared through the ivy. Ra followed with Henry puffing behind.

"Katy…………..Katy will you stop for heaven sake."

Katy slowed and then came to a halt.

She turned and looked at Ra who had stopped to catch her breath. Henry had plonked himself on floor panting.

"I'm sorry I don't know what came over me. Here have some squash. Henry do you want some water. Henry sat up waiting.

Ra sipped out the bottle as Henry slurped out of the bottle of water.

"Katy I do get the impression that you like that beach but it's there for everyone to enjoy."

Katy nodded and smiled. She still couldn't explain why she had reacted the way she did. She placed the two bottles in the rucksack and they carried on back home.

Dusk was beginning to set in when they got home. Henry went into the kitchen to his bowl and slurped at his water. Ra disappeared into the living room and plonked herself in her chair. Her legs were aching but she did feel like she'd had a good day.

"Would you like a hot drink?"

"Yes please."

A few minutes later Katy walked in with two cups of hot coffee.

She sat down by the table and placed the drinks on the table.

Ra looked over and smiled.

"That beach is very beautiful how did you find it?"

"I'm not quite sure. If I remember Henry disappeared through the ivy bush and even though I could hear him I couldn't see him. So I just followed through and after struggling to get through the hole in the rocks the beach appeared. "

"It was very peaceful I have to say. "

Katy smiled and drank her coffee.

The room was quiet. Ra began to wonder why Katy had reacted the way she had when the boat appeared.

The sun had now gone and the moon was glowing onto the garden. Ra could feel her eyes closing.

"Think I'm of to bed."

She took her cup into the kitchen and placed it in the sink.

Katy sat looking out onto the garden.

Everything was quiet and still.

12

Ra lay looking at the ceiling. Not something she did that often. She felt a little nervous but couldn't understand why.

She looked at the clock. Fancy being awake on a Sunday at 6:45am. Henry was fast asleep. She turned on her side and looked out of the window. It was to early to get up and she was going to struggle to get back to sleep.

Outside was quiet. Suppose everything else was still fast asleep.

She looked at the clock it was 7:30am.

"Well I can't stay here I'm going to have a shower. "

Henry lifted his head and then lay back down. Ra stepped quietly passed Katy's room and into the bathroom.

The shower was lovely and warm she could stay here all morning. She headed back towards her bedroom to find Henry had moved from his own bed onto hers. His head was comfortably embedded in her pillow. Ra smiled as she dressed. Henry wasn't taking a blind bit of notice.

Ra headed to the kitchen and put the kettle on. She still couldn't understand why Katy had reacted the way she did when the boat appeared.

She headed into the living room and sat in her favourite chair. It was now nearly 9am a more sociable time to wake up on a Sunday. It was all quiet outside but beautiful.

Henry appeared at the door wagging his tail.

"Well good morning sleepy head I suppose you want your breakfast?"

Henry turned and went back into the kitchen. Ra followed and went for his biscuits. Another cup of tea would be a good idea she thought. She looked down the hallway to see if Katy was coming but all quiet.

Bring bring, bring bring. Ra turned and headed into the living room.

"Hello. Oh hello how are you? What today no ive not really got anything planned. Oh ok I'll come over in about an hour if that's ok. Alright see in a while."

Ra put the phone down and turned towards Henry.

"Millie says she has some important information for me so we'd better drink up and pop over. What do you think?"

Henry huffed and began to tap his paws with excitement. Ra finished her breakfast and quickly washed up.

She stopped outside Katy's room but could hear nothing.

Henry stood by the front door waiting for his collar to be put on.

They disappeared down the lane towards Millie's.

It felt a little chilly even though the sun was out. Birds were chattering away which made Ra smile.

"Well good morning fancy seeing you here."

Ra jumped as she looked to her left. Andrew came from the left with a sort of spring in his step.

"I wonder what information she's found out. It would be good if it helped us close the investigation don't you think?"

Ra looked and just smiled.

They arrived at Millie's door and knocked. Henry stood behind them.

The door slowly opened.

"Well hello come on in."

Millie led them to the front room. There was already a pot of tea with 3 cups on the table already.

"Come on sit yourself down."

They both sat as Millie poured the tea.

"James called me last night to say he had found some information that could help you. He's going to drop it in this morning on his way through. I did ask him what it was but he said we'd understand when we sore it."

Ra looked puzzled what information would help them. They didn't know the name of the boat or the family.

"Let's hope so. We know that the disappearance of the daughter could have something to do with that Spanish boat but without the name of the boat or the family were stumped. "

Andrew looked at Ra and nodded.

The doorbell rang and Henry jumped up and started barking. Millie left the room and headed down the hallway.

"Thankyou I'll see you soon. "

Millie came back in with an a4 envelope. She looked over at Ra and Andrew. Who should she give the envelope to? She passed it to Andrew.

He pulled out some papers and began reading. The room was silent.

"Oh dear."

"What's the matter."

"Well we know the name of the daughter who disappeared. We have the name of the boat. There was even a book written about the boat. It says that the book will tell us all we need to know."

"Well that's good so where do we get the book from. Is there one in the library?"

"That's the problem. There was only one book written and it has never been seen."

"Well what was the name of the girl?"

"Well the girls name was Harriet Jane Teagle locally known as Katy and the boat was called The Princess Clipper."

Ra felt the colour drain from her.

"Ra are you ok you look like you've seen a ghost?"

Ra looked over at Millie.

"I'm fine just feel upset about the poor girl at what she went through."

- Ra looked up at the clock on the fireplace. She wanted to go home but couldn't be seen to rush. She wanted to see Katy and ask about the book. How could it be she had the only copy of the book.

Millie and Andrew were talking but Ra didn't hear a word they had said.

"Well that's it then. So near and yet so far. I really thought we would solve it."

Ra looked over at Andrew.

"Maybe it's true what Mr Ridge said. It was a mystery that was never meant to be solved. "

Andrew shrugged his shoulders and finished his tea.

"Well if it's ok with you both I'm going to head back home. I want to clear my shed."

Ra stood up said her goodbyes and left. She walked quicker than normal and Henry was panting as he followed.

Within 15minutes Ra was opening her front door.

"Katy hello are you up?"

She headed towards her bedroom and opened the door. The room was empty and the bed was made. She headed into the living room nothing, then to the kitchen nothing. Ra rubbed her head.

Where had Katy gone. She looked towards the back door and there it was on the table. Ra walked to the table and picked up the book. She turned it over. The Princess Clipper. She flipped the pages until she got to the back. She noticed the last page felt a bit thick. She pulled at the corner and the page came away. Underneath was a folded piece of paper. She pulled it out and opened it out. It was a map. What was this.

She went to close the book and noticed some writing on the last page.

        IM HOME NOW

Printed in Great Britain
by Amazon